# Homegoing

# Homegoing

## A NOVELLA

by

Toni Ann Johnson

Accents Publishing • Lexington, Kentucky • 2021

Printed in the United States of America

Accents Publishing
Editor: Katerina Stoykova-Klemer
Cover Collage:
Waterfall: © Dominick Fiorille
Church: © FBC Monroe, NY
Woman: © Leonard Chang
Skyline: Deposit photos free images
Photoshop: Kevin Rock

Library of Congress Control Number: 2021937155
ISBN: 978-1-936628-66-7
First Edition

Accents Publishing is an independent press for brilliant voices. For a catalog of current and upcoming titles, please visit us on the Web at

*www.accents-publishing.com*

*For Len.*

# I

*New York City, 2006*

"Hi, Maddie. How are you? It's snowing up here. Can you believe it? Jesus, I hope it doesn't stick. How's the weather where you are?"

"It's—"

"Oh-oh, I'm glad you called. Listen, I got somethin' to tell you. Remember Mr. Ferrell? From down the hill? Bought that civil war saber from me? Remember? Y'there?"

"Yeah," Maddie said.

"Well, why didn't you say something?"

"'Cause you don't—"

"Shh, shh, Listen, listen, he *died!*"

This was typical. As her mother aged, she barely let Maddie part her lips, and she was obsessed with the obits. She read them daily. Compulsively. Even casual acquaintances knew that if you bumped into Velma at the Stop & Shop, you were in for an updated litany of the dearly departed locals.

Maddie was wearing pajamas. In the middle of the day. She was curled up like a fist on the floor beside her upright piano. She couldn't say she was moved by Ferrell's passing. The man had never been nice to her. His kids hurled rocks and racial epithets when they were growing up. She hadn't seen him since the mid-eighties—twenty years ago—and he'd looked old *then*.

Nonetheless, she exhaled and said, "That's too bad, Mom."

"Yeah. So sad. All my contemporaries are either *going-going* or *gone*." Velma chuckled at the auction quip that made regular appearances in her "*you'll never guess who died*" routines.

"Rolando's moving back to L.A.," Maddie told her. "He doesn't want to be married anymore."

"Oh," Velma said. "Sorry to hear that." Then her voice brightened to a higher key. "Weeeell, so you'll be single. So what? *I've* been single for over twenty-five years now, and I love it. I'm glad I don't have to deal with your father's bullshit anymore. You seen him lately? Jesus, he looks old. Like an antique. A relic. Like I could sell his ass in my shop ..."

No matter the content of the conversation, when her mother was participating, its focus would be on her.

Velma went on complaining as Maddie set the phone down and climbed off the floor. She shuffled in her fleece and corduroy slippers, hunched against the cramping in her abdomen. With the bathroom door open she peed with the light off and stared out the doorway so she wouldn't have to see her lady parts cry blood. Across the room, boxes were stacked like giant bricks, making a wall along the windows: a stroller, a breast pump, an infant tub … She closed her eyes and blindly replaced the pad with a fresh one.

When she made it back to the phone Velma was still monologuing.

"… and you know he was so damn cheap, honestly, when I wasn't working after I had you, he'd give me a few dollars spending money, and then he'd make me go buy *him* cigarettes and scotch with it. What an S.O.B." Finally, she asked, "So what happened, anyway? Why doesn't Ro wanna be married anymore? Another woman?"

"Uh … He said—"

"Y'know, just because you make more money doesn't mean you should always be the boss. Rolando told me you control everything and you *do*. You get that from your father."

Ouch.

Why did she always hope her mother would be different? She wanted to say, *fuck you*. Instead, she bit her tongue. She bit the crap out of it. She'd need stitches if she bit it any harder.

"Y'there?" Velma asked.

"I'm hanging up now."

"Oh, you don't wanna talk, huh? Well, all right, then. You'll be fine."

For a moment, Maddie imagined her mother sounded caring, the way one might encourage a toddler to come down a slide. *It's okay. You'll be fine.* "Really?" She sniffled. "How do you know, Mommy?"

"Because what choice do you have, Maddie? Life goes on. Until it *doesn't* and you read about in the paper!"

A couple of days earlier, Monday morning, they'd been fifteen weeks along. Rolando and Maddie sat across from each other in their kitchen nook, arguing about moving to a larger apartment in the building. A sharp tug in the gut folded her over. A red puddle spread between her legs and across the white bench.

At the hospital he didn't want to see her. He wouldn't look. Maddie kissed her tiny head and said goodbye. Her name was Nina. She fit in the palm of her hand.

They left in a taxi without her. Maddie couldn't speak. At a stoplight, the sun wandered through the window and swirled in her lap. She was dazed, watching it shimmer there, when Rolando's fingers gripped her thigh so hard she yelped.

"I'm sorry," he blurted. "I can't stay here anymore." His lashes were clumpy with tears.

By Saturday Maddie's breasts remained sore and engorged, and she still needed a maxi-pad. Her abdomen cramped occasionally, though less than it had. From the bed, messy and crinkled as a pile of dead leaves, she watched her husband pack brown shipping boxes in their white-walled studio on lower Lexington Avenue. He hadn't slept there during the week. She didn't know where he'd been, but he came by for an hour or so each day to pack, and to purge, and he'd brought her soup each time, even though she barely spoke while he was there. She couldn't. Her head ached and her mind had been gone—nowhere and elsewhere—trying to find the dimension that takes in unborn souls.

On a typical Saturday, they'd be playing a CD—Ella, Miles, or Monk—or she'd be at the piano practicing while Rolando edited photos on his laptop. They'd chat over the music.

It was quiet now, except for the creak and rip of packing tape and the cars whooshing by outside. Above the stack of unopened boxes, windows that stretched to the ceiling lined the east wall facing the street. They welcomed a gray November day inside. It seemed to hover in the room like a melancholy ghost.

The place was large for a studio, but it was only one room, which made it difficult to opt out of watching Rolando dismantle the remnants of their life together.

He was tall and broad-shouldered; muscular like an athlete, though he hadn't been one since college. His hair was short and only slightly kinkier than Maddie's. Hers was past her shoulders. They were the same shade of golden-light-brown. People often asked if they were siblings. Nina would have looked like both of them.

"You gonna get ready for work?" He kneeled on the Turkish rug across the room. His long fingers held the flaps of a box together as his other hand pulled tape along the seam.

Maddie's hair was a matted nest, and she was in the same black pajamas she'd worn since Monday night. She'd been asleep more than awake. She hadn't slept like this since the childhood depression she'd suffered after being molested by a sitter during a family vacation abroad. When you can't change something and you can't live with it either, there's sleep.

Her hands clutched her empty belly like a keepsake. "I sent them an email. I'm not up to singing yet."

"Still? You said the cramping was better. You need to get out and do something."

Maddie sat up in the bed and stared at him in a way that searched his face. Ransacked it.

His amber eyes winced, and his forehead inched backward as if her gaze spooked him. "What?" he asked.

"What are you doing, Rolando?"

"What d'you mean?"

"Are you packing?"

His head tilted as he regarded her with cautious hesitation. "Ye-ah."

"Leaving? For good?"

Rolando exhaled and eyed the ropey fringe at the edge of the rug.

"I know you feel guilty, but don't pretend you're concerned about my wellbeing."

He pushed himself up with a grunt and thudded across the parquet in his Timberlands. He sat beside her, his lower body twisted, so his feet touched the floor. He draped a heavy arm across her back. It pulled the fabric of her pajama top tight against her breasts and it hurt. *Everything* hurt.

"Of course I care. But things haven't been cool for a while. A baby would've made them worse."

"She had a name."

He lifted his arm, turned toward his feet and leaned forward, elbows on his thighs. His fingers entwined beneath the square chin she loved looking at. He stared out the balcony's glass door at the brick building across the street. "It's not working for me, living in your world that I can't afford, doing what you decide. This is *your* life. Mine's not happening here. Have you been concerned about *my* wellbeing?" He stood.

She grabbed his sturdy hand and squeezed it. "I wanted her," she said. "I really did. Maybe it seemed like she was more important to me, but—"

"*You* wanted a baby. You pressured me to go along, even after what I told you the first time. You knew I wasn't ready."

"We waited almost a decade, Rolando. I'd be in menopause if we waited any longer."

"Yup." He yanked his hand from hers. "It's all about

you."

The pounding behind her eyes was so robust it felt like her heart had scaled its way into her skull to see what the fuck was going on. "I wanted you, too," she said. "I tried to take care of you."

"In the way *you* wanted to do it. I never wanted to move here."

"And I didn't want to stay in L.A. dealing with your parents. I did that for you. For years."

Rolando leaned down into her face. "And I've been *here* all these years." His teeth were clenched. "We're even." As he thunked back toward his packing boxes, he shook his head. "You need a shower, girlfriend."

Rolando grew up in Baldwin Hills, where they met when he was twenty-nine and she was thirty-three. Maddie had a recording gig, singing backup, and he'd been hired to shoot photos of the session. She was supposed to stay a week. After a year, they married. She played clubs and did backup vocals and jingles before finally returning to New York to do a friend's musical at The Public Theater. She was forty-three now. Her FSH level was high. They'd done IVF twice.

"She was my last chance."

He started on another box. Sneakers and shoes. He didn't look up.

"You can still have your own, Rolando. With someone else."

"Stop talking to me," he said through closed teeth.

She wanted to throw a tantrum, to scream, cry and stomp around hurling stuff at him, but her head was throbbing and whatever fire she'd had in her was snuffed out. She hunched over to the sofa and clicked on the TV. She flipped through channels. On CNN, a voice shouted from the screen, startling her: "Shut up! Fifty years ago we'd have you upside down with a fucking fork up your ass. Throw his ass out. He's a nigger!"

Rolando's head popped up in Maddie's peripheral vision.

Michael Richards, the tall guy with the troll doll hair who played Kramer on *Seinfeld* was on stage at the Laugh Factory yelling at a Black heckler.

"He's a nigger! He's a nigger!" Richards shouted. "Look, there's a nigger!" The audience gasped.

"Oh, shit," Rolando said as he stood up from his box.

It was hard to watch and hard *not* to watch. As she sat on the sofa, her pulse quickened and the inside of her ribs ached. The outburst triggered memories of kids in her neighborhood who'd called her that word. She remembered the adults, too. Especially mean old Sally Gore who said it at the school bus stop. "Reminds me of home," she said. "Monroe was the deep north."

He walked over and stood behind her. They watched Richards babble and curse. The Black man yelled, "That was uncalled for." And Richards was screaming again. Then he mocked the guy in a tone that seemed to Maddie like he was trying to sound Black. "I don't know," became, "Aah don' know, Aah don' know." As people in the audience got up to leave, bodies blocked the camera intermittently.

Rolando leaned over her, snatched the remote, and changed the channel. The same video appeared. He clicked to another channel and a correspondent said Richards' outburst happened the night before in L.A., and that it would likely kill his career.

"Guess I'm done watching *Seinfeld*." Rolando muted the TV. "Who knew Kramer was in the Klan?" He dropped the remote in Maddie's lap. "Don't keep listening. Y'know they're gonna run that crap over and over. It's bad for the soul. And I'm not playin', you should really take a shower." He went back to his box. The packing tape *eeeeeeeked* as he pulled it off the roll.

She pivoted toward him. "I don't know *what* you're talking about, Larry."

His eyes racked focus to hers. His lips curved into a smile that quickly dissipated. His face quivered. "C'mon, don't." He took a breath, eased it out, and finished sealing the box.

They had their own patois. Words. Phrases. *I don't know what you're talkin' about, Larry*, came from a boxing match they watched on HBO. Larry Merchant interviewed Lennox Lewis after a beatdown by Vitali Klitschko. Lewis technically "won," because Klitschko was injured and they stopped the fight. The audience booed. Larry rightly implied that Lewis looked like a punk in the ring and that Klitschko should've won.

Lewis said, "Pshh. I don't know *what* you're talkin' about, Larry."

The denial. The arrogance. Palpable enough to taste and so delicious they chewed it up like Cheetos.

The morning after the fight, Rolando complained about the eggs she'd made. "Too runny," he whined.

She looked at him and said, "Pshh. I dunno *what* you're talking about, Larry."

He keeled off the nook bench cracking up. And the phrase was added to the "Roladdie" lexicon.

He stacked four boxes on a beat-up, two-tiered gray cart by the door, then rolled the batch out. She unfolded herself and crept over to the window to watch him exit the building, four floors down. What if she dove through the glass and landed—splat—in front of him?

He loaded the boxes into a rented white van parked out front. When he finished, he rested one hand on the back door and leaned into it as if catching his breath. She watched as he stood that way for a while. Then he slid the sleeve of his hoodie back and forth across his eyes. Maddie wanted to hug him. She wanted to punch him. She wished he would stay.

When he came back in he walked over and plucked one of his framed black and white photo prints off the wall. He plucked another. There were more than twenty of them around the room. She faced the TV. He was behind her. She heard him stack the prints onto his rickety cart. When she finally turned around, he'd gotten them all down, except the one he shot of her the week they met. He left that one. She watched him wrap a couple of prints in pages of her *New York Times* and place them into the box on the floor.

"I haven't read that yet," she said. "Did you ask to use my newspaper?"

He eyed her without stopping and said, "Sit back, Polly."

Another Roladdie phrase. This one came from a movie. Jude Law was flying a plane and Gwyneth Paltrow, *Polly, not* flying the plane, was trying to tell him how to do it. Bossy. So Jude's character told her, "Sit back, Polly." Rolando and Maddie often *sit back, Polly-ed* each other in lieu of saying *shut up, stop bothering me.*

In her photo, the one Rolando wasn't taking, Maddie is standing on Sunset Boulevard in Hollywood, the sun lighting her long, dark curls from behind. She seems younger than thirty-three. That's because she's happy, looking at him and giddy in a terrified way, knowing she's about to take a leap even if there's no net there to catch her.

An unframed picture of the ultrasound at fourteen weeks was taped on the wall above the oak chest of drawers a few feet from her photo. Nina looked like a peanut with a shell. Moments earlier, she and Maddie were accompanied by Rolando's other photographic mementos—places he'd traveled, friends, random objects that intrigued him, like coffee cups, shells, and park benches he featured in shadow or light or both. Now it was just Maddie and the peanut.

"The walls look barren," she said.

His back was to her, as he used the cart. "Can't you just be quiet? Please."

"It wasn't my fault. We could've tried sooner. We should have."

Facing the cart, Rolando leaned on its edges with both hands. "Look, I've only got an hour to get my shit to the UPS Store and return the van." He went back to wrapping the photos.

She hugged her knees to her swollen chest and turned sideways. Her bare toes squeezed the edge of the sofa arm. "Why did you have to fight me that day? I wasn't asking you to pay any more rent than you already weren't paying half the time."

He swung toward her. "Shut up, Maddie."

"You scared her with all your yelling and complaining."

"You lost the baby 'cause you're too fucking old to have one!"

She didn't flinch. Her eyes pushed back at his. If he thought he could crush her more than he already had, she'd disappoint him.

He turned and wrapped another print, tender with it, careful, as if diapering a baby.

The TV was still muted when she looked again. On Fox News, Greta Van Susteren was interviewing Paul

Mooney at The Laugh Factory about Michael Richards. Maddie's back was to Rolando and his to hers.

"Even if we'd had it," he said, "I would've had to leave."

"Her name was Nina."

"I have to make my own way."

"We made her. You act like you had nothing to do with it."

"I don't wanna be dependent on you, Maddie. What don't you understand about that?"

She turned to find him facing her. "You stood in a church and promised *for better or for worse,*" she said. "Why? So that ten years later you could leave to go get your shit together? So, what, your *next* wife gets the improved version?"

"Stop it. This isn't about a *next.*"

"Fuck you. If you didn't want to be dependent you should have found a real job."

"How would you feel if you had to get a real job?"

"I've had plenty of them, Rolando! What do you think I did until I could support myself singing? I didn't have a sucker wife to pay my bills."

He gusted out a breath as if blowing dust off a camera lens and then gave her his back again.

"I can't afford alimony," she said.

"Oh. But you were gonna be able to afford a baby? Okay." He sealed the last box.

"And don't ask for it, 'cause I'll add up all the rent and

bills you never paid and you'll end up owing *me*."

He took a Sharpie from his hoodie pocket and wrote "FRAGILE" on the box.

"I'll hurl myself off the balcony before I give you any more money."

Rolando eyed the ceiling. "I've had my mail forwarded to my parents'," he said. The bluster had petered out of his voice. "If anything comes, write 'return to sender' if you don't wanna deal with it." He pushed the cart, set his keys on the glass entry table, and opened the door. When he looked back, his eyes lingered on her a bit longer than they should have. "So long, Maddie," he whispered. His cart rattled as he rolled it into the carpeted hallway.

She raised the volume on the TV so she wouldn't hear the sound of him closing the door for the last time.

"Throw his ass out," Richards yelled. "He's a nigger! He's a nigger! He's a nigger! A nigger! Look: there's a nigger!"

The first time that word happened to her, the Ferrell boys chased her and her best friend Tobias, and threw stones from their driveway at them. Maddie wanted to believe she'd been worthy enough to be Rolando's wife. And Nina's mother. During the past week, she'd struggled to convince herself that she *did* have value. She added something to the world. She deserved to be here. But the word that told her she was nothing, no one, hurled through time and hit her like a rock.

Days later, the doorbell rang, waking her. The blinds were closed, electronics unplugged, and it was black hole dark in the apartment.

"Maddie?" It was her mother's voice. She pounded on the door, THUD THUD THUD. "Are you in there?"

She stood, and then tottered. The room was a swaying boat.

"Oh my God," Velma said when Maddie opened the door. "You look half dead." Velma stood there in her long black mink. Her dark eyes winced, and then welled to a sheen. "Jesus." She hugged Maddie tight.

Maddie was not a fur fan. She donated to PETA. But the cool softness of Velma's coat was silky and soothing as she nuzzled her cheek in it. Velma's frame seemed smaller, more delicate than it had a couple of months earlier. Maddie thought she might break her if she squeezed too hard.

"My baby," Velma said. "It's just a man." She moved inside, set her Coach bag and tote on the entry table, and then she tugged Maddie into the room by her hand. "Get out of those pajamas. I'm running you a bath." Her heels clicked onto the hexagon tiles as she stepped into the bathroom. Maddie heard the water flow. Velma stepped back out. "I said, get out of those filthy pajamas, Maddie. You smell like a bag lady. How long have you been like this?"

Maddie lifted and dropped her shoulders.

Velma put her hands on Maddie's cheeks and looked

at her, mouth agape, horrified. She felt her forehead.

Velma's bronze skin was barely wrinkled, despite her age. The full face of makeup—foundation, powder, mascara, eyeliner, shadow, and lipstick—was too much, but the beauty she'd once been hadn't faded much.

Woozy, Maddie's right hand grabbed the piano for support. The left one grabbed the antique chest of drawers. Her wedding band clacked against the wood. "What are you doing here?"

Velma opened the closet and slid Maddie's clothes aside to hang her coat. Maddie imagined sad little animals screaming from the hanger.

"You haven't answered the phone all week," Velma said, pushing up the sleeves of her cashmere turtleneck. She gave the contents of the closet the once-over before she closed the door and turned to Maddie. "You were supposed to meet me at your grandparents' today. It's Thanksgiving. My God, your face looks gaunt."

"Thanks."

"Pale, too. Have you eaten today?"

Maddie shook her head.

"There's food in my bag. Get in the tub. I'll fix you a plate."

When her pajamas came off in the bathroom, Maddie thought the mirror would shriek if it could. Velma was right. Her face *was* gaunt. Her hair was a frightening mess, too. She hadn't noticed because she'd never turned the light on in the bathroom and she hadn't undressed.

Her stomach wasn't back to flat yet, and her breasts were still engorged, but her face, arms, and thighs were thin like they hadn't been since she was a teenager trying to starve her backside off so it would look like the white girls' she went to high school with. She'd barely eaten since Saturday when Rolando was there. She slept most of the previous day and couldn't remember eating at all.

"Ow." Her foot burned as it entered the tub. She eased the rest of her body down into the scalding water anyway. The heat seemed to make her organs seize inside. Could she be cooking them? The pain was oddly pleasurable. Interesting. Maybe because she hadn't felt much of anything except numb for a while.

Her mother marched into the bathroom and thrust a large glass of water at her.

"Drink this," she said. "You're probably dehydrated." She hovered above Maddie and made sure she finished it.

"I'm sorry you spent the day alone, honey," she said. "You'll come home for Christmas. Your grandparents are going to your cousin Suzy's, and I don't feel like traveling way out to Connecticut."

Maddie handed her the empty glass. "Thank you."

Velma closed the top of the wooden toilet seat, sat, and unzipped her black leather boots. She set them outside the open bathroom door and then cracked her toes. "What's with all the baby stuff?" she asked, eyeing the boxes by the windows across the room. There was a wild glint in her eyes when she whirled toward Maddie.

"You're not pregnant, are you? He left you and *you're pregnant*?" She shook her head. "You must have really pissed him off."

"I'm not. For fifteen weeks I was. Now I'm not."

Velma's fully made up face froze for a moment with her mouth open. "And you didn't think to tell your mother?"

"I'd planned on doing it today. Thanksgiving would've been sixteen and a half weeks. Last time we miscarried at twelve. I wanted to be sure."

Velma huffed out a sigh. "You shouldn't have waited 'til middle age." She examined her bare nails. "I was thirty-one when I had you. That was considered old then, but I was a lot younger than you are. I didn't have any problems."

"Do I not seem sufficiently miserable to you?"

Velma's pencil-enhanced brows crinkled. "What?"

"Telling me it's my fault and how you did it better is not comforting."

"Oh, Jesus, you're so sensitive, Maddie. I didn't come all the way down here to be scolded."

"May I have some privacy, please?"

"For what? You don't have anything I don't have and I didn't come all this way to sit by myself."

"I'm still passing blood and bits of tissue. Could you *please*?"

"Elwl. Why? Is that normal?"

"What do you mean, *why*? What did I just tell you?"

"All right, all right." Velma stood. "Why're you yelling? Calm down."

Maddie put on a black velour sweat suit, twisted her wet hair to one side, and ate Thanksgiving leftovers at her round oak table with the chatty shrinking lady who seemed intent on inducing her mental breakdown. Plate filled with collard greens, candied yams, Jamaican rice and peas, turkey with gravy, mac and cheese, and whole-berry cranberry sauce, it smelled sublime. Her first real meal in days.

"You've got too much furniture in here," her mother said, looking around. "But the chest of drawers does look good by the piano. I didn't think it would."

Maddie spoke with her mouth full. "Glad you like it."

Velma looked over her head to stare at it. She fingered the back of the walnut brown curls she had colored every few weeks at the one salon in the Monroe area that could do Black hair. "But why don't you polish the drawer pulls? The brass is dull. You need to brighten 'em up."

"They're bright enough for me," Maddie said.

"That piece came from an old customer. If I hadn't seen her obituary, I wouldn't've known about the estate sale." Velma got up and padded over to the bureau in her stocking feet. She ran her fingers along its top, and then she leaned in to stare at the ultrasound photo taped on the wall above it. After a moment, she padded back and sat down. She looked at Maddie's plate. "Well? You haven't said anything. You like it?"

"Everything's good. You made the baked macaroni?"

"Don't I always?"

"Especially the baked macaroni. Delicious."

"Good."

As Maddie ate, she watched Velma turn and squint at the photo of her that Rolando left by itself on the wall.

"Why don't you hang some art or something? These empty walls are depressing. I have some prints in the shop I could give you." She turned back to Maddie.

Maddie met her eyes and glared a moment before she said, "You have nothing to say about the ultrasound?"

Velma leaned back in her chair and floated her palms open. "What's there to say? I was almost a grandmother. And now I'm not. I'm not gonna feel sorry for myself. You don't get everything you want in life. But you make the best of it."

Maddie rested her fork. "You think this is *your* loss?" She laughed, not because it was funny, but because it was so very Velma.

"It's funny that I'll probably never have grandchildren?" She crossed her arms across her chest. "No one to visit me for the holidays like all my friends have? Thanks."

"Mom, you don't even *like* kids. And thanks for coming to check on me only to remind me how disappointing I am."

"I never said that."

"You're not a grandmother. So what? Did you get to be a mom?"

"What's your point?"

"Did I?"

Velma fingered the corner of the placemat in front of her.

"You don't get to make me feel guilty right now," Maddie said.

"I wasn't trying to do that." She looked up and stared at Maddie's left hand. She gave a nod to the platinum wedding band. "Want me to sell that for you?"

"You know what? I'm full." Maddie got up and carried her unfinished plate to the kitchen.

Velma's eyes followed her. "You're not throwing that out are you? Cover it up."

"Would you stop?"

"What? I don't want it to go to waste. Oh, I meant to ask you, you used to watch *Seinfeld*, right? I never watched it, 'cause there were never any Blacks on it. But did you see what that guy did? It was all over the news. Awful, wasn't it?"

"Yeah, I saw." She covered the plate with aluminum foil.

"He says he's not a racist. He apologized to Jesse Jackson and Al Sharpton. Sharpton refused to accept."

Maddie trudged back to the table and slumped into her chair. "Of course he's a racist."

"What do you think about Sharpton not accepting

the apology?"

"Would you?" Maddie picked a piece of lint off her velour hoodie.

"I don't know." Velma stared off at nothing discernible. "If I thought it was sincere, I might. If someone's willing to change, I think you should be willing to let them."

"Huh. I'd sure love to hear apologies from all the people who called me the N-word in Monroe."

"Oh, Maddie, all *what* people? You act like you lived through Jim Crow. It wasn't that bad."

"Mom." She leaned closer until they were eye to eye. "I've traveled the country. I've traveled the *globe*. And the only place I've been called the N-word was in that red-state territory you and Daddy called home. And it happened so many times, I would've needed a fucking adding machine to keep count."

"Stop exaggerating."

"I'm not. And I was expected to shrug it off. People didn't apologize or lose their jobs or status back then. They relished saying it and there were no consequences."

"Well, you certainly didn't complain to me about people saying that to you all the time."

"'Cause you didn't give a damn about what happened to me."

"Well." Velma closed her eyes. She exhaled and her lip trembled. "I can see you don't want my company." She stood.

"I *tried* to tell you when that neighborhood witch

Sally Gore said it to me at the bus stop, and when that girl's father said it when we were in junior high when she asked if I could come to her house, and when one of the mothers said it at ballet. You never wanted to hear it."

"I'm going to go catch my bus. My little Bertold is by himself and I should get home before he does his business in the house." She sniffled.

Maddie rose and followed Velma as she plodded toward her boots that were sitting outside the bathroom door. "In third grade Rick Moore, a ferret-faced moron who'd known me since kindergarten finally figured out that I was Black, and he wanted to make sure everyone knew."

Her mother stopped moving. Maddie spoke to her back.

"Every day, when we lined up to go to lunch, I stood behind him. And each day he turned, and loud enough for the other kids to hear, he said, 'You're a nigger.' I was the only Black kid in the class, one of less than a handful in the whole school. And—"

"You think I don't know that?" Velma turned. "Who do you think put you in the school, Maddie?"

"I'm not finished."

"It was a good school." Velma crossed her arms and eyed the gold bracelets on her wrist.

"For a few days in a row I told Mrs. Keener what he said, and she kept him inside at recess. That meant she was stuck in the classroom, too. By the fourth day she growled at me in her mean, pack-a-day voice, 'CAN'T YOU JUST IGNORE IT?'" Maddie leaned close to her mother's face the way Mrs. Keener had leaned into hers.

Velma stepped back. "Well, you should have told me. I would have gone up there and spoken to her. But you've got to put this stuff behind you."

"She might as well have slapped me. And ferret-face kept it up. I tried to ignore it. Then more kids started doing it. That bitch knew, and she didn't do shit. Did it ever occur to you that I would've been better off being around more Black kids?"

"Listen, I grew up with plenty of Black kids." She turned away to step into her boots. "And lemme tell you, they're every bit as mean as white kids." She zipped them up and then opened the closet door. "I had to switch junior high schools because three girls came to my house and threatened to cut my face over some boy who thought I was pretty."

"Cousin Suzy never got beat up and she lived around Black kids."

Velma slipped her mink off the hanger, slid into it, and faced Maddie. "Well, your cousin Suzy wasn't as pretty as I was. And you weren't the only one who had a hard time in Monroe. You had Jewish friends who got picked on."

"They had each other, Mom. They all went to Hebrew school at Monroe Temple. I didn't have anyone."

"That's ridiculous. You had friends in Monroe. You still have friends there. Don't you talk to Liser all the time? And Julyer?"

"I didn't have anyone who was *like me*."

"Oh, so what? I didn't have anyone who was like me growing up, either. They made fun of Jamaicans. Called us 'monkey chasers.' I survived. And so did you."

"Go get your bus."

"And Suzy didn't have all the things you had—trips abroad, piano and voice lessons, tennis lessons, a swimming pool. You had more than most of those white kids you grew up with, too."

"Bye, Mom."

"You turned out all right," she said.

"Are you serious? You said I looked half dead and smelled like a bag lady!"

"But this'll pass. I was a wreck when your father left, too. I wasn't making enough money. I was suicidal. *Homicidal*, too. And your uncle Aubrey gave me a gun. Okay. The *only* thing that stopped me from killing your father was that I knew you'd never forgive me. And he's damn lucky, too, 'cause I was—"

"Mom!" Maddie opened the door. "Go. Take care of your mean little dog."

"Don't badmouth your little brother." Velma kissed Maddie's cheek. With her thumb, she wiped the lipstick she'd left there, and then stepped into the threshold. "If you get lonely, you can always come home."

Maddie shuddered. A turkey-scented draft blew through the hallway. "Being lonely's not so bad." She hugged her shoulders.

Velma's eyes puddled. "Why don't you come for the weekend, Maddie?"

"I have to work."

"Well, at least come for Christmas so we won't be by ourselves. I'll call you later."

Maddie watched her mope down the hall until she turned for the elevator.

# II

Saturday, she was back at the piano bar. Old-school, wood-paneled, and dark, it was in the lobby of a hotel long past its heyday. Maddie played the old Steinway and sang Ellington's "In a Sentimental Mood," a song about some happy fucker bragging about being loved. Performing it heartbroken gave it an edge.

She saw her dad slope in wearing his mid-length black leather coat and his kooky, matching fedora, looking like Shaft, straight out of the seventies. Phil's hair puffed out on the sides in curls dyed too dark for his seventy-four-year-old face. His diamond-stud earring glinted as he cut through Maddie's spotlight and bumped into an empty barstool before sitting on it and ordering a dry Rob Roy in the kind of voice people at the gym use when they talk while listening to music with headphones on. He turned to watch her, saw that she was looking at him, and he waved.

Then it started.

Phil's roving eyes scanned the crowded room. He came in to see Maddie sing, which was sweet. He also came to check out women, and sometimes he hit on them. And it was every bit as cringe-worthy as a daughter would expect.

Coltrane's "Lush Life" flowed from the speakers when she took her break and squeezed in at the bar to stand beside him. Her father kissed her cheek and patted her back. White stubble on his face scratched her cheek.

"That dress looks good on you kiddo. You lost some weight."

The clingy dress was black cashmere. Maddie rested her hands on her shrunken hips. "Thanks, Dad. I'm underweight now, but I know you like your women emaciated."

Phil smirked and flicked his manicured hand, to dismiss her dig. His current girlfriend was about as thin as a cigarette, and as white as one, too. "And your voice sounds better," he said. "Less shrill on the high notes."

"Oh. I didn't realize I was shrill," Maddie said. I'm *not* fucking shrill, she thought.

"Sometimes." He nodded. "On the high notes."

Sergei, the beefy bartender set his drink down in front of him and dropped a cherry into it.

"What the hell is this?" Phil asked.

Sergei raised his chin. His nostrils flared. "It is Rob Roy," he said, rolling his "Rs" in his Russian accent.

"I *told* you I wanted a *dry* Rob Roy," Phil said, raising his voice. "It's made with *dry* vermouth, not sweet."

"Agh," Sergei growled, and snatched the drink back.

Phil looked at Maddie. "What's wrong with that guy? I order the same thing every time I come in here and he always gets it wrong."

"I work here, Dad."

"I'm a paying customer, Maddie," he yelled. "He needs to get it right." Phil stretched his neck to watch as Sergei picked up the dry vermouth. Then he turned to her. "Your mother told me about your, uh, uh …"

"Of course she did. You two chat a lot for people who can't stand each other."

"I'm sorry for your loss, kiddo." He squeezed her arm.

"Thank you."

"It's a dark time. I know. But things will change." He patted her back again and then turned to look over his shoulder at the room.

He was fairly well put together, she thought, in a tan lambswool turtleneck under the leather coat. The red silk scarf was too much, though.

"Where's your friend Sam tonight?" he asked.

Maddie let out a loud exhale. "Sam's gay. She's not gonna go out with you."

"Huh," Phil grunted. "She sure flirted with me last time."

"Dad. No she didn't. She's just friendly."

He tilted his head and smiled. "*You* don't think your father's anything special. But, y'know, women think I'm in my forties."

She gave him a dubious look. "*I'm* in my forties. No, they don't."

"You'd be surprised," he said. His voice was brimming with confidence. "I've got more young women hitting on me …" He stared off. A sly grin on his face suggested an especially fond memory.

"*And* you have a girlfriend," Maddie said. "Remember her? What's her name?"

His smile fell away. "No one asked you to police my relationships."

"Well, good for you," she said. "No one's hitting on me. I've got nothing going on."

Sergei slid a new Rob Roy in front of Phil and gave Maddie her usual: a tall glass of water, no ice. He winked.

"Thank you for putting up with us, Sergei." She smiled.

"Your father is grumpy old man," he said.

"Old? Well, guess what?" Phil snapped. "I'm senile, too. So don't be surprised when I forget to tip you."

Sergei snorted and hulked down the bar to another customer.

Phil sipped his drink and held still a moment, tasting it. After a slight nod of satisfaction, he looked at her. "Try not to be too down about the marriage," he said. "I've had two of them, my sweet. They come, they go. Someone else always comes along."

"Maybe. But Rolando understood me."

"Understood what?"

"Me," she said. "How I was damaged by my upbringing."

Phil snorted. "Oh, right. The never-ending *woe is Maddie* saga."

She sliced him with her eyes. "He went to all-white schools, too. He knew what I went through."

"Maddie, you're middle-aged now."

"I'm aware. You've been pointing that out since I was thirty-five."

"Think your childhood was tough? You're not unique. All day long I treat people who say their childhoods were tough."

"And do you tell your patients to get over it?"

"When it's appropriate, yes. Dwelling ad nauseam on your unhappy past will not yield a happy present."

Her fingers gripped the edge of the bar. "I try not to," she said, staring at her hands. The left one seemed to taunt her, naked without its wedding band. "But it formed me, Dad. When you're always the outsider, you end up thinking you're meant to be alone."

Phil sighed wearily. His eyes roved. And landed.

Maddie turned to look. Shit. There she was: Sam, a spectacularly beautiful Malaysian woman, sitting at a table, by herself in a low-cut, black jumpsuit. Wavy dark hair cascaded to her waist. She was slim. Golden skin. Late thirties. Maddie watched her father watch Sam as if she were a glass of premium scotch he was eager to savor.

"That's your destructive drive talking, Maddie," he said. "Your *destrudo*. It's what the psyche does to attack itself. I talk about it in my book. You're breaking yourself down, instead of building yourself up. Stop those thoughts." His eyes were still on Sam. "Stop telling yourself how terrible life was, and is."

"It *is* terrible, though."

"Because you keep telling yourself that." He smiled. Not at Maddie. At Sam. He waved as she acknowledged him. "Yes, your marriage ended. And there's no baby. Of course those losses are painful, and you'll grieve. But you can make new connections and new experiences, and you can focus on things that are good. Think forward, not back. Imagine happy times in your future. Create them in your mind. Pursue them. That's your constructive drive, *construdo*. With construdo you build your life up, instead of breaking it down." He finished his drink with a gulp, pulled a ten and a five from his money clip, slapped them on the bar and stood up. "Have a good set." He squeezed Maddie's shoulder, straightened his back as upright as it would allow, and he strutted off toward Sam.

Maddie hiked herself up onto his barstool. She did not watch what was about to unfold.

Sergei took the money. "Your father is asshole," he said, and laid a meaty hand on top of hers. "But, he give you good advice." His gray eyes twinkled. "Be happy. Make yourself a good life."

"Thank you, Sergei. I liked the one I had. And I can't

see my future. Maybe I don't have one."

"Don't die," Sergei said. "Then you have future." He took a cherry and plopped it into her water. "Let good things come."

Christmas Eve after they exchanged gifts, at his place in Greenwich Village, Phil gave Maddie a ride upstate. He drove his third Mazda RX-7 since the seventies. This one had an itty-bity back seat and his dog Sasha, a clingy Doberman, was nestled into it, looking out the window. Phil wore a full-length fur.

"I can't look at that coat without imagining little otters being clubbed in the head," Maddie said.

He was chewing gum, which he did a lot since he'd stopped smoking. "They shoot them. They only club them when shooting doesn't completely kill them."

"Oh, great. Thanks. That's even better."

"I know you hate fur, my sweet. You grew up in a very different time. When I was a boy in the Bronx, after my father died, my mother told me that we were now poor. Then one day I was walking home from the corner store, shivering, in a thin coat, my nose running from the cold, and I saw a beautiful open car with two young white couples, all of them in fur coats, probably raccoon, and they were smiling, enjoying themselves, looking like they sure knew how to live. Told myself one day *I'd* have a nice car, a pretty lady, and a fur coat, too."

Maddie thought he looked like a pimp in that coat,

but she kept it to herself. "It's nice that you got the things you wanted, Dad. At least one of us did."

He patted her head. Behind her, the dog yawned.

"Thanks for the ride. Glad I don't have to take the bus."

"You used to like the bus when you were a teenager, going to your lessons in the big city." He smacked his gum. "You were so excited when you could finally go by yourself."

"I was excited to be getting out of Monroe. The fumes nauseate me now and sometimes I run into people I'd rather not see."

"Mmm," he said. "You were right about Sam. She's not into men."

Maddie blinked and focused on the taillights of the car in front of them. She didn't want to know how he came to that conclusion and she prayed he wouldn't tell her. She changed the radio from classical WQXR to WBLS, urban adult contemporary. An R-Kelly song was playing.

"Ack, no," Phil said. "Not this. You wanna change it, put on NPR."

"I want to see if my jingle comes on."

"Oh? What jingle?"

"I recorded a McDonald's spot back in the fall. It's running now."

"Fantastic." He patted her head again. "Congratulations."

"Wanted you to hear it."

"It's coming on now?"

"Not sure, but it might."

"Might? Make me a recording." He changed the station back. Beethoven's 7th.

"McDonald's didn't think I was shrill."

"And since you've got so much money, you can give me some for gas." He laughed.

As they crossed the George Washington Bridge, she stared out at the Hudson below. "I heard six people jumped this year."

"Yeah?"

"Wonder what that would be like?"

"What?"

"Think it hurts?"

"What are you talking about, Maddie?"

She rested her forehead on the window. Sasha put his head on her shoulder.

"I know you're feeling down, kiddo, but this is just temporary. You'll find another relationship. And then if you want a baby, try again."

"It's ten thousand dollars for another IVF cycle. I've had two miscarriages. Would you invest with those odds?"

Sasha bathed her cheek with his tongue. It was icky, but so sweet she petted his snout and didn't complain.

"You can adopt," Phil said. "And you don't need a partner."

"And be a single parent?" She shook her head.

"Then enjoy your life without kids. They can be a pain in the ass."

She turned and looked at him. "Thanks. That really helps."

He stared at the road.

"I wanted to give Nina what I didn't have."

Phil groaned. "You had everything, Maddie. Try being grateful. How about that? And get back into therapy. I'll put you in touch with a colleague of mine. You should make an appointment with her. Soon."

"Sounds great. Is she someone you've slept with?"

He side-eyed her. "Never you mind."

Maddie banged the back of her head into the seat.

Phil and Velma still shared the property they bought in the seventies, even though they'd been divorced since the eighties, and it had been on and off the market for twenty years since then. It was near Walton Lake and not too far from where they rented when they first twirled into town with their youth, dreams and good looks, and people threw eggs at them. Velma lived in the main house, and Phil used one of the two cottages as his part-time office. Their buildings were separated by the pool, landscaped grounds, and the tennis court. They each had their own driveway and almost never had to see each other. Sometimes he stayed the night in his cottage, though not this night, because he was meeting his so-called girlfriend, who lived in nearby Chester.

Velma's Dachshund, Bertold, barked as she opened

the door in her bathrobe and slippers, and let Maddie into the foyer. As she set her bags on the floor beside the entry table, Maddie saw no evidence of Christmas.

"Where's your tree, Mom?" She eyed the spot near the living room where it should have stood.

Velma puffed the air out of Maddie's down coat as she hugged her. The dog growled. "Shh. Quiet, Bertold," she said.

He barked. It was high pitched and annoying. Maddie watched him waddle-dance around her in angry circles on his stubby legs.

"Ugh," she said.

"Oh, he's ok," Velma said. "I didn't wanna deal with the needles and all that nonsense. Too much of a bother. I'm getting up in age, Maddie. How do you think I was gonna manage carrying a tree in here by myself?"

"What about a fake one?"

The dog, still barking, sounded something like a seal to Maddie. Kind of how she imagined Julia Child might have sounded when she coughed. *Aurph, aurph, aurph*!

"Bertold, quiet," Velma said. "I have pine-scented candles. That's Christmas-y enough."

"All I smell is this stinky dog. Is he gonna stop?"

"Aurph. Aurph."

"Shut up, already," Maddie shouted.

He raised his snout and bared his tiny yellow teeth at her.

"Something must be wrong with him, Mom.

Dachshunds aren't supposed to smell bad."

"Aurph, aurph."

"Leave him alone," Velma said.

"You have to bathe him once in a while."

"Aurph, aurph, aurph!"

"You just worry about bathing yourself."

"I'm going to bed. Merry Christmas," Maddie said.

"Aurph, aurph, aurph!"

"Merry Christmas, love." Velma kissed her, and the dog *grrred*. "Glad you're home. First time I've had you for the holiday without Rolando in ten years." She sighed.

"Aurph, aurph. Aurph, aurph, aurph!"

"Bertold, that's enough," Velma said.

"Goodnight, Mom." Maddie grabbed her stuff and trudged down the hall. Bertold followed, stinking and *aurphing* in his high-pitched doggy voice. She felt something grab and pierce her calf.

"OW." As she spun around, the dog lowered his head and walked backward, growling. "He bit me!"

"What?" Velma stepped into the hallway and shook her finger. "Bertold, bad boy! Bad dog!"

"That's it? You're just going to yell at him?"

"What do you want me to do, Maddie?

"What would you do if he bit *you*? What would you do to *me* if *I* bit you?"

"What? You want me to hit him?"

"Since when do you have a problem with that? You had no problem beating the crap out of *ME*."

"Stop yelling," Velma said.

"Aurph, aurph, aurph!"

Maddie yanked a *Newsweek* magazine from her bag, rolled it up, and whacked him on the head. He yelped and cowered. "Bite me again, you smelly cur, and I'll throw your little ass in the lake." She whacked him harder.

"Maddie!" Velma's eyes were brimming with tears. "Stop it, now. That's enough, you hypocrite. Aren't you supposed to love animals so much?" She snatched Bertold up and cradled him like a baby. "You're frightening him—he's just a little dog."

"He bit me, goddammit." Maddie twisted back and pulled up her pants leg to find a red wound with teeth marks already swelling. "Look what he did to my leg!"

"Well, you must have provoked him."

"I didn't do anything to him. I was walking away. Don't cuddle him, yell at him!"

"Bertold is my companion. You'll go back to the city and all I'll have is him. Did it break the skin?"

"YES."

"Well, put some peroxide on it. You'll be fine." She walked away, carrying the dog. "I'm sorry she did that to you, my poor sweet baby," she cooed.

"You're a barking lunatic just like he is."

Maddie's old room had the same single bed and antique white wicker rocking chair that had been there since she was a teenager. Her leg stung as she set her stuff down on the carpet, looked at herself in the wall mirror, and silently asked why she kept subjecting herself to this shit. Her last shrink told her she had "self-defeating personality disorder," which meant she was a masochist. Maddie had refused to believe it at the time. She stormed out of the office and didn't return. Now, as she stared at her own reflection, what was blindingly obvious stared back.

The next morning Velma had curlers in her hair, and she was making coffee in her vintage percolator when Maddie limped into the kitchen. The dog was lying on the floor, wearing a red Christmas sweater that said "Santa Paws" on it. He lifted his head and growled.

Maddie stuck close to the door. "Put that dog in another room," she said.

"What?" Velma didn't turn to look at her. "Just ignore him, he'll be fine."

"My leg is still throbbing, Mom."

"Well, put some antibacterial ointment on it."

"Get that dog out of my sight or I'm calling a cab."

"Aagggh," Velma scoffed, and faced her. "You make everything so damn difficult, Maddie."

Maddie's face burned. Hot, unshed tears stood their ground as she glared at her mother.

Finally, Velma scooped Bertold up, and stomped out of the kitchen. As the percolator gurgled and hissed, and the smell of coffee pervaded the room, Maddie heard her feet bang up the stairs toward her bedroom.

Later they sat in their sweat suits sipping French roast and vanilla almond milk in the white-tiled kitchen that, aside from the refrigerator and dishwasher, hadn't been updated in close to thirty years. The round oak table (like Maddie's in the city) had been Velma's since she began collecting antiques back in the sixties. The caned chairs pressed their pattern into Maddie's sweatpants.

Velma held the *Times Herald Record* in front of her face. "Hmph. Isn't that interesting?" she whispered to herself. "All the years I knew her ... had no idea."

"The obituaries again?"

"Don't bother me," she snarled.

Maddie set her mug down. "Mom, y'know, what we focus on inevitably shows up in our lives. That's why I wish you wouldn't read about death every day."

Velma leaned her head full of curlers from behind the paper, sucked her teeth, and said, "Maddie, please." She turned the page. Seconds later, the paper still covering her face, she added, "So, I guess *you've* been focusing on divorce then, huh?"

Maddie wanted to whack her with a rolled up magazine. "No," she said," gritting her teeth. "But *you've* been talking about yours for the past twenty-five years. I couldn't escape it."

"Oh, I see," Velma said. "So it's *my* fault your husband left you."

Maddie took a breath and squeezed her cup so tight her fingers ached. "You know what? Read them all you want. I don't care."

"What're you afraid I'm gonna die?" Her pink curlers peeked over the top of the paper.

Maddie sipped her coffee. She felt something hot and hopeless welling inside of her. "Not really. I may go before you."

"Well, I did stop taking my Lipitor. Made my ankles swell." Velma lowered the paper to look at her. "Y'know you really gotta be careful with these damn medications. They'll kill you."

"You stopped taking your cholesterol medicine?"

"I feel fine."

Maddie sighed. "Did you tell your doctor?"

"I said I feel fine."

"There are no symptoms, Mom. It doesn't matter how you feel."

"Well, I don't give a shit. I'm not taking it anymore." Velma leaned toward her. "And what do you mean you'll go before me?"

Maddie stared into her coffee. "What do you care?"

"Of course I care."

"You said yourself your dog is more important to you than I am."

Velma set the paper on the table. "I didn't mean it like that. You're too sensitive."

"You said it. And you did mean it." She gulped the rest of her coffee. "How'd you get to be a mother and I didn't?"

Velma hitched her shoulders up and down. "Younger eggs, I guess."

"I have no reason to be here."

"Reason?" Velma looked her in the eye. "Why 'cause you lost your husband? Please."

"And no kids."

"Eh—there's plenty to live for without kids. Lots of people do it."

"And my career's not what I wanted it to be."

"Maddie, your career's not over. *Make it* what you want."

"It's not like I'd be missed."

"Oh, would you stop feeling sorry for yourself. I'd miss you. You're my baby."

"Yeah. The baby you let your dog bite with impunity." She stood and carried her coffee mug to the percolator beside the sink.

"Make sure you turn that off when you empty it."

"Really?" Maddie spun toward her. "I'm too stupid to figure that out?"

"Well just don't leave it on ... You'll find another husband."

"*You* didn't."

"I didn't want one, Maddie. Listen, you've got it much better than a lot of singers. You make a living at it. Perk up. You've got it better than a lot of people, period. And whining won't fix anything. When I went through a divorce, I didn't whine about it."

"Oh my God. Yes you did. Endlessly." Maddie eased into the chair and blew on her coffee.

"I did not. Even while I was fighting your father, and believe me, that was a fight, I buckled down and I made my business a success. I took courses to learn more about antique jewelry and I cultivated an expertise." Velma looked over Maddie's head like she was giving a speech and directing it to someone in the last row of an auditorium. "I learned more about advertising. Rearranged the store. Trained myself to be better with customers. Stopped telling them to get the fuck out when they pissed me off. And when they assumed my white employees were the boss instead of me, I set them straight politely, no attitude. I nurtured my business, until I had confidence that I could take care of myself." She pounded the table with her fist. "I've done damn well without a husband. Who needs one?" Velma smiled. Then she looked at Maddie.

Maddie looked at her.

"Oh, I know what we can do that's fun," Velma said. "We'll drive into town later when it gets dark. I have to drop a gift off at the Megners. You can visit with Liser and then we'll look at all the pretty lights and decorations around the old neighborhood. I love seeing them."

Maddie sipped her coffee. "Lisa emailed me. She's in Jersey with her husband's family. Say hi to Iris, but I'm not going into town to look at anything. Why would you think I'd enjoy that?"

"I don't know." Velma's shoulders slumped. "Just thought maybe you would."

"No. *You'd* enjoy it, because you like it here. You love the quiet, and the trees, and the Republicans, and the racists. I'm not you."

Velma stared into her empty mug. She tapped her nail against it, making a bell sound. "Well, I'm sorry you're so unhappy, Maddie. I don't know what to tell you. Maybe you need to talk to someone. I talked to someone when your father left and it was very helpful."

"Yeah? Well you should know, my last shrink told me I should limit contact with you."

"What?" Velma's head jerked back. "I don't believe that. *Why*?"

"I'm serious. She said you're emotionally immature and a toxic narcissist."

"Psh. That idiot didn't know what she was talking about."

Maddie took the bus back to New York the next day. The day after that, as she arrived to fill in at the piano bar for the other singer who was on vacation, Velma called on her cell.

"Hi Maddie. How're you? It's warm up here today. How's it where you are? Listen, I—"

"It's warm here, too!" Maddie shouted into the smartphone. Her way of reminding her mother that a phone conversation was between *two* people. "Almost sixty degrees."

"Oh?"

"Crazy. Climate change. It's scary."

"Oh, everything scares you, Maddie" she said. "Listen, I've got some bad news—"

"Let me guess. Someone died." She hung her sweater in the coat-check room.

"Yes." Velma sighed. "Iris Megner."

"What?"

"Heart attack."

Maddie batted aside some lost and found scarves and leaned against the paneled wall. Something invisible had pushed her in the chest.

"She was fine Monday night," Velma said. "Can you believe that's the last time I'll see her? We go back forty-three years."

"I'm sorry, Mom. I loved Mrs. Megna."

"See? You should've come with me. At this age, some of us, y'know, we just expire."

Iris was their next-door neighbor when they lived in town. Maddie remembered how she always had a smile for her when she went over to play with Lisa. She was welcoming and kind. Her last name was Megn*a*, with an "a." The "er" at the end was Velma's New York accent.

"I'm gonna miss her," Velma said. "My garage sale pal. We had good times."

"Lisa called you?" Maddie asked. "She didn't call me."

"No, Lis*er* didn't call me. She's probably too upset. It

was in the paper!"

Of course it was.

Maddie hung out with Lisa after Tobias dumped her for the neighborhood bullies. When her cousin Suzy visited, she called Lisa "Peppermint Patty-Lisa," because of her red hair and freckles. The name eventually whittled down to "Patty-Lisa." She drove them both bananas with questions about their Black hair. But Lisa was never mean. She didn't call Maddie names, even when they argued.

Before her set, she approached Sergei at the bar. "Hey. Could you ask your uncle if I can have this Sunday off to attend a funeral?"

Sergei crossed his massive arms. They seemed especially muscular in his tight, white collared shirt. He squinted at the ceiling a moment, as if he were thinking, and then he nodded. "Probably it's gonna be okay," he said. "Because I'm manager while he's take holiday. Tonight you help us out. Of course. We get someone Sunday." He nodded again. "Don't worry yourself, beautiful." He reached out his thick warm hand and patted hers.

"Thank you. Let me know," she said. "'Cause if you don't find someone I won't go. I had to pay a lawyer to file the dissolution documents, and Rolando could still request spousal support. I can't afford to get fired."

"That guy." Sergei shook his head. "Someone should break his legs."

"Sergei. Why so violent?"

He scoffed. "To break heart is violent. Take longer to heal than legs."

Maddie saw something behind his pearl gray eyes that she hadn't noticed before. She squeezed his hand.

The hotel was at capacity for the holiday week and that night's early show was crowded. Maddie added "Autumn Leaves" to her set, because in the fall she, Lisa, and Lisa's brothers used to jump out of a maple tree into piles of earthy-smelling leaves in their backyard, while Mrs. Megna laughed and took Polaroids. She made them hot cocoa after. The lyrics were about missing someone, in particular, a lost love. Maddie dedicated the song to Mrs. Megna, though she couldn't help thinking about Rolando. And Nina, too.

As her eyes closed, Maddie's tears drenched her lashes and spilled onto the keys. Her voice was unwavering. When she was new to singing, it used to catch and crack when she cried. With practice she learned to keep her throat relaxed, and to focus her thoughts ahead of what she was feeling. If she set her mind on what was coming next, she was less overwhelmed with the emotion in the moment. The strain wasn't there and sound glided out with no resistance, as easily as tears.

She heard, "Sing, girl."

Maddie opened her eyes to see Sam, her dad's crush, smiling at her. Oh, how she dreaded the conversation they would have about him. Sam lived on the top floor of the hotel. She often traveled for work. When she was in town, she regularly graced the bar with her presence, filling the room with her beauty and bright, charismatic energy like a deity. Sometimes she stayed late and hung out with Maddie after her set. She talked about her love life. Her last girlfriend had not only cheated, she also once spit in Sam's face during an argument. That someone as strikingly gorgeous, accomplished, and seemingly together as Sam could find herself mistreated in love was unfathomable to Maddie.

On her break she waved and Sam joined her at the bar. The woman was a study in simplicity and elegance, stunning, with barely any makeup, just a touch of mascara and lip gloss. Her long hair was twirled into a loose bun. She wore diamond studs, a black cashmere V-neck, and tan wool slacks with heels. Maddie stood. As they hugged, she felt Sam's fingers on her bare back and smelled a hint of rose-scented perfume.

"Happy holidays, Miss Madeline," Sam said. "Fucking magnificent. I mean it. Quite moving." Her accent was more English than her native Malay. "Why're you in this wee little spot and not on Broadway?"

"You're sweet. Where've you been?" Maddie said, sitting back on the leather stool.

"Working like an indentured servant in Brussels." Sam cozied up beside her. "I designed two hotel suites in the time I typically do one."

"Brussels sounds fun, though."

They eyed each other sideways.

"Brussels is lovely," Sam said. "Didn't see a lot this trip. It's lovelier to be back. And to see familiar faces." She stared at Maddie for several seconds. Smiled. "It gets lonely being in cities where I haven't got friends."

"I was worried you'd stopped coming in because of my crazy father. So sorry about that."

"Oh, don't be." Sam giggled. "There's something rather charming about him."

"Ugh. Hope you didn't tell him that."

"He has quite an ego, though, hasn't he?"

"Sorry."

"It's fine. I admire his geriatric swagger."

Maddie's shoulders crept toward her earlobes—cringing.

"So tell me, how are you, Madeline?" Sam asked. "Feeling okay?" Her hand stroked the skin on Maddie's arm.

"I guess." As Sam's fingers traced the bluish-green veins between her wrist and elbow, Maddie stared at her friend's short perfect nails with their light pink polish. She hoped her skin felt smooth. It was strange to be touched this way by a woman. It gave her goose bumps. Maddie turned her head and sipped her water with no ice.

Sam reached up and touched Maddie's chin with one finger. She turned it toward her until Maddie's eyes met hers. Then she was silent for an uncomfortably long pause—Maddie counted twelve beats—before Sam said,

"I've been worried about you."

"Uh, what?" Maddie felt her face flush. "Why?"

"Am I going to have to kidnap you?" Sam asked.

"Me?" Her arms were glistening with sweat now. She felt tipsy, too, though she was not imbibing. She glanced at Sergei. His gaze shot heavenward, pretending, badly, that he wasn't interested. "Why would you want to do that?" Maddie asked.

Sam swiveled on the stool to face her. She placed her hands on Maddie's bare shoulders and turned her body toward her own. Their knees were touching. Maddie's were barely covered in sheer stockings. She could feel the soft wool of Sam's pants tickle against her skin.

"Last month your father told me you've been isolating. And tonight you wept through your songs. Maybe you need company? An ear?"

"My father talked about *me*? While he was with *you*?

"He did. After he called me exquisite. And asked me to dinner. And I told him I'm into women, and he said 'Oh, I'd be into that,' and I explained I meant *only* women, and he said 'Have you *tried* men?' and I sighed."

Maddie leaned out of Sam's grasp and covered her face with her hands.

"Then your father said, '*Y'know*, I was only in my teens when Maddie was born.'"

"Oh my God." Maddie peeked through her fingers.

"And I laughed," Sam said. "Then he laughed. And I said, *sir, please stop*. And he finally said, 'Okay.' That's when you came up. He said you hadn't been reaching out to anyone, just going to work, and otherwise withdrawing. He was worried. I am, too." Sam folded her pretty hands in her lap. There was an intensity in her eyes that unnerved Maddie. She imagined Sam was using a magnetic force to draw what she wanted to her.

"Thanks, Sam. I'm ..." Maddie stopped. She was about to cry and she didn't want to. She shrugged and shook it off. "I'm getting by. Just in between lives, I guess." As Sam caressed Maddie's arm again something fluttered inside her. "There's uh, um ..." *Christ*, she thought. I'm stammering. "Probably something y'know, I'm supposed to, uh, *do*. Here. In this ... liminal—whatever—existence, but I don't know *what*."

"Grieve?" Sam said, her voice low and husky. "And heal?"

There were tears on Maddie's face, she realized, as Sam reached up and wiped her cheek with a cocktail napkin. And then she stood. And then she hugged her, pressing her body against Maddie's. There was more fluttering. Sam's embrace was a security blanket. Safe. But *more* than that. Her hand caressed Maddie's back and the way she stroked it was definitely ... *Wow*, Maddie thought. She didn't know this about herself. The last and only time she was with a girl, some thirty years ago, she was inexperienced and she didn't like it, or the girl. But she didn't not like *this*. She was pretty certain Sam would kiss her if she offered her mouth. Could she be misreading things? Why would Sam want *her*? She wasn't gay. She wasn't young. She wasn't ridiculously beautiful like Sam was. Sam could do better. But Sam did not let go. In fact, she squeezed Maddie tighter and kissed the side of her face. It felt welcoming. Seductive. Both. She was pressing her chest against Maddie's and Maddie was filling with giddy amazement realizing that if she were not in public and at her job, she'd totally tongue kiss this woman. Then Rolando popped into her head. Dammit. Why? Why did she feel guilty, as if she still belonged to him? What a waste of all the agony she'd been in over *not* belonging to him anymore.

Maddie felt Sam sink her fingers into her curly hair. A surge of anxiety followed. There was a tug on her scalp as those fingers got stuck, trapped in the inevitable tangle. If one dared to plow through Maddie's field of coils, proper tools were needed—a pick or wide toothed comb, and water or detangling spray. And you had to start at the ends, not the scalp. Maddie sighed and leaned back to see Sam's impossibly long-lashed gleaming eyes on hers. Sam was smiling with a tightly closed mouth as if to keep a laugh from escaping. Her hand was still imprisoned by the kinks.

"Black girl problems," Maddie said.

Finally, Sam *did* laugh. With her mouth closed. It was high and squeaky and sounded like a cat meowing. Maddie laughed, too, as she guided Sam's hand out of her head. Then she saw Sergei glowering at them. This stifled her laughter. And not only that, a few middle-aged men at the other end of the bar were staring. A balding, white guy raised his beer glass at them. *Cheers*.

"I don't want to be a spectacle," Maddie said. Her stomach churned.

"Shh." Sam kissed her forehead.

Maddie breathed deeply. Though she didn't dislike whatever it was she was doing with Sam, she didn't want to do it here. Over the years, she'd been hit on at the bar. She knew how to deflect advances deftly, without losing a fan or a customer. It had been easy then—she was married.

With her freed hand, Sam kneaded a spot on Maddie's neck at the base of her head, and her body responded by tingling, everywhere, as it anticipated what would come next. Massages had been in Rolando's seduction toolkit, too. She couldn't believe this was happening.

"Your father is here," Sergei barked.

Maddie looked at him.

He thrust his fist-sized chin toward the entrance.

She turned to see Phil standing in the doorway in his leather coat and his kooky black fedora, his dyed curls sticking out. He was gaping at her. And at Sam. His gobsmacked expression puckered into that face he made when a bartender fucked up his drink. Maddie groaned softly.

"Dry Rob Roy. Dry vermouth," Sergei said, his voice rising above the hum of bar noises, chatter, and of Ella singing Gershwin.

Phil marched toward the bar. Maddie and Sam untangled themselves as he approached and stood directly in front of them. He smiled. "Well. How're you girls doing?" he said, oozing with phony cheer, as if he hadn't been scowling just a moment earlier.

"Hi, Dad." She didn't know what else to say.

Sam was composed. "Delightful to see you, Dr. Arrington." Before he could respond, she turned to Maddie. "I must pop upstairs for a bit. I'll try to hurry back before your set is through." Her lips curved into a smile. Her eyes, however, glinted tensely as if to say *fuuuck*. No way was she coming back that night.

Maddie and Phil watched her glide away. When she disappeared through the door they looked at each other. His jaw was tight, face gritted into a growl. He took Sam's seat. Sergei set the Rob Roy in front of him. He crossed his arms and stood there, watching them like a play.

Phil threw back a gulp immediately. Then he turned to her and barked, "Did you call that psychologist I recommended?"

His tone went too far. Maddie stared at him for several seconds. "It's *the holidays*," she said. "And, like you said, I'm middle-aged. I'm grown enough to schedule my own activities, professional or otherwise." She descended from her stool and headed back to the piano.

Phil left before her second set was through.

Sam had her number. And Maddie didn't hear from her the next day. Or the day after. She had Sam's number, and her email, too, yet she didn't get in touch either. If Sam wanted to connect, she would, Maddie figured.

She took extra care with her hair and makeup for the rest of the week. Sam never came into the bar. Sergei pretended not to notice the false eyelashes, the frizz-free tendrils she tamed with a skinny curling iron, or how deflated Maddie was each night by the end of her first set.

She decided she'd be okay. After Rolando and before Sam, even in her dreams, *sexual* dreams, she was alone, trying (and failing) to pleasure herself. At least now she could imagine being with someone again. Maybe. Someday.

# III

Sunday, New Year's Eve, Maddie pulled herself and her bags toward the queue for the 3:10 to Monroe at Port Authority. Exhausted from hiking up and down subway stairs and carrying an overstuffed suitcase and a backpack, she got in line. To keep from seeing anyone she knew (or being seen), she kept her face in her Palm Treo and engaged in self-torture, looking at old photos taken with Rolando. They both seemed happy in them. Even a bad marriage has some good memories. Did *he* miss anything?

"Maddie!"

Dammit. She lifted her head, and there was a man ahead of her in line looking back and waving a burly hand. There *was* something familiar, though not enough to recognize him. Behind the guy was a Black man, bespoke, in what looked like a camelhair coat and a Kangol cap. Their eyes connected. She smiled. He nodded the way Black people in places with nothing but white people tend to do. Was he really going to Monroe? She wondered. And if so, why?

The waving man's hair was a black-silver ombré

that covered his ears. His dark, rectangular eyebrows reminded Maddie of piano keys. He stepped out of line and his feet clunked down the concrete floor toward her in work boots.

"Hey," he said.

She squinted, still trying to place him.

"No way. You don't recognize me?" he said.

Maddie heard a twinge of hurt feelings.

"Sorry," she said.

Hand to his chest he leaned in. "It's Toby."

"Toby?"

"Tobias."

"Oh. Wow," she said. "Really?" Something lurched in the pit of her stomach, like her guts had seized. Her heartbeat began to pulse in her neck.

"Hey, buddy," he said.

She exhaled, blowing out what felt like fear, the kind she'd felt back when he was hurling insults at her.

His teeth overlapped slightly in front. His smile was sizable and it seemed to send warm energy swirling all around her. Or maybe she was having a hot flash. She hoped she didn't seem too shocked. He was different from the last time she'd run into him. Not *terrible* different. Older. Heavier. Weathered.

Tobias. Breaker of her young heart.

She exhaled again. "I was just thinking of you not long ago," she said. It was true. He'd been on her mind since the Michael Richards rant.

"Long time, huh?" he said. "Too long."

"Yeah. Since the eighties." Maddie's stomach now felt like it was falling off a roof. Not fluttering. Anxious.

"I remember," he said. "In Hoboken. The Path Station."

He wore a tan bomber jacket, a plaid flannel shirt, and jeans. His arms opened. She hugged him. Massive shoulder blades on his sturdy back filled her hands like boulders. His scent brought her back to high school and their bus stop on the corner by the waterfall.

"Is that your father's cologne?"

"O-oh. This is like a dog greeting, huh?" he said, letting her go. "Wanna sniff my butt, too?" His voice was more playful than sarcastic.

Her cheeks rose.

"Made you smile." A laugh honked out of his nose. "You're totally right, though. I'm stayin' with the old guy."

"Oh." *Living at home?* she thought. *Yikes*.

"Temporarily." He leaned in for emphasis. "My Maaad-die," he chimed, singsong-y, like he used to when they were little kids. His eyes clung to hers like magnets. He adjusted the Lands' End backpack slung on his shoulder. "Goin' to Mrs. Megna's funeral?"

She nodded. "You, too?"

"Whoa," he said, noticing her stuffed suitcase and backpack. Hers was leather. "How long you stayin'?"

"Couple of days." She rolled her head around. Her

neck and shoulders hurt from lugging so much stuff.

"The hell you got in there?" he asked. One black piano key brow shot above the other. "Cases full of potions? That how you stay so young?"

She thought she might be blushing. "One day it's warm, then it's freezing. Wasn't sure what I'd need. So I brought everything."

"Ya never need as much as you think."

The line chugged forward toward the bus. Tobias grabbed the handle of her suitcase and rolled it for her. When they approached the luggage compartment, he lifted it inside with a grunt.

"Gee Manetti," he said. Then he slipped two fingers onto her shoulder under the strap of her backpack and he carried it aboard for her.

When had he cultivated such genteel manners? He certainly wasn't chivalrous when they were teenagers and he was regaling her with fine phrases like, "Disco sucks," as if, because she wasn't white, she was responsible and made the damn music herself.

He stowed his backpack and hers above a seat several rows from the front. His chin flicked toward the window, telling her where to sit. This was teetering on the edge of bossy, though his intention seemed sweet. She sat and breathed through her mouth to avoid the bus fumes. The Kangol cap guy was a row ahead and diagonally across from them.

Tobias plopped himself down with a weighty sigh, as

if it had been a long, taxing day. It was only a few minutes past three.

"Something wrong?" she asked.

He rubbed his face with his hands. No wedding ring. He was married, last she'd heard. "Been a tough couple of months," he said.

"Mm," she replied. She didn't tell him they had that in common.

As the bus moved out, she removed her hat and loosened her down coat. Sweat beaded on the back of her neck. Her mouth felt dry.

"I live in Astoria," Tobias said. "And I'm workin' construction, assistant foreman, down at ground zero, but I been commuting from Monroe lately 'cause pop has brain cancer."

The news stunned Maddie like a Taser. "Oooh," she said, almost wailing.

"Yeah. Won't do any treatment."

Maddie squeezed his lower arm. "Why?" Her voice rose a couple of octaves and made the Kangol guy turn around.

Tobias shrugged. "It's not gonna save him. He's got a few months. Symptoms aren't that bad yet. Fatigue. Bit of memory loss. That's okay, though, 'cause some of his memories were effed up anyway. He forgot we didn't get along." His eyes were sorrowful, even as he managed to lift the edges of his lips into a smile.

Maddie always hated to see Tobias in pain. She put

her hand on his. "We're at that age."

"Are we? Naw," he said. "Not you. You still look like a kid."

"Thanks. Black don't crack."

"'Scuse me?"

"You've never heard that expression?"

His head swiped left, right. *Nope.*

Of course he hadn't.

"But beige do age!" Kangol-man said from across the aisle, adding, "Apparently, not in your case, though."

Maddie and Kangol-man laughed. Tobias's raised brows suggested he was confused. Kangol-man turned back to face front.

"Melanin, Tobias. It keeps us looking younger than, y'know, *most.*"

"Huh. Well, it's workin' for you." His eyes glided over her. "Keep it up."

She snorted.

"What?"

"Can't really 'keep up' my melanin. It is what it is. But, thank you."

"Well, don't get a big head, 'cause since I hit forty I really can't see shit."

"Ah," she said. "Should've known." She took her hand back. "You did call me ugly—among other things—when we were kids."

"Well." He scratched his nose. There was a little dirt under his fingernail. "C'mon. Kids are assholes. They say all kindza things."

"Mm hm," she said. "All kinds of really mean things." She looked out the window. It was rattling and tapping, the wind playing it like a drum. The bus had just come through the Lincoln Tunnel and it was pushing into Weehawken. Manhattan's skyline gleamed across the Hudson.

"Hey," Tobias said. "Remember the time you flashed your lil' boob at me and Bob Grout in the lunchroom?" He wheezed a laugh.

She turned back to him willing her eyes to spit darts.

"You don't remember that?" he said. "Third grade? Lisa was there, too. You had on a tank top. Zippo underneath."

Her cheeks and upper lip began to perspire.

"You grabbed your shirt, tugged it to the side ..." He grabbed his jacket and pulled it to the left. "And ta-daa! A little surprise popped out. That was great."

"Remember when you called me an ugly nigger?"

Kangol cap spun back toward them, eyes wide as Tweety Bird's.

"Whoa," Tobias said, wincing as if he'd been pricked by something sharp. His jaw went slack and he deflated, hissing out what seemed to be every last bit of his breath. "Where'd that come from?"

"You're bringing up things *you* remember."

"Jeez."

"Well? Do you remember?" Maddie fanned her face

with her hand.

"No. I didn't think of you like that."

"Tobias." Her chin dropped to her chest and her heavy lidded eyes came at him with the force of a shove.

"What? I didn't. You were just my friend."

"We stopped being friends in first grade, because you—"

"Because I was a *boy*, Maddie. I stopped playing with girls."

"No."

"Yeah."

She crossed her arms. "Remember when you banned me from spin the bottle?"

"What?"

"In seventh grade. DiPrima got sick. Our class was unsupervised. The kids played spin the bottle and *you* told everyone *I* couldn't play. When the kids asked *why* you said, 'She knows why.' Well, I *don't* know, Tobias. If you didn't think of me *like that*, then why?"

He shifted in his seat. Stretched one leg into the aisle. "I don't remember that."

She sucked her teeth. "I stood outside the game near the door while the rest of you played."

His face turned purplish pink. "Maybe you had a cold sore. I dunno. Or maybe I didn't want anyone to kiss you, 'cause *I* liked you."

"Bullshit. No, you did not. You called me ugly. Bubble butted. And you *know* what else."

He hunched over and massaged the crease between his brows with his middle finger.

"Are you flipping me off?"

"No!" His eyes stretched open all the way as he turned. "What *I* remember is when we were little you were my best buddy. Maybe I didn't appreciate that as we got older, but that's 'cause I was a doofy, thickheaded boy, not 'cause you were Black."

They sat quietly for a while.

"Really. So you're denying what you said?"

"I don't know. I didn't even think of your family like … I didn't see color."

"Stop." Maddie's hands flipped into the air and plopped back into her lap.

"You barely even look Black."

"Just stop."

"I'm telling you … what *I* remember is eating snack cakes, drawing with Crayolas, playing on the tire swing, and down at the club in that nasty brook when our dads played tennis. The kiddie pool. Badminton. We had fun. And I remember you sticking up for me when Bobby and Kevin Ferrell teased me about my dad's disability."

"Yeah. I did." She held his gaze.

Her eye contact, which was relentless, seemed to ruffle him. "What?" he said, his voice impatient.

"Did you *ever* stick up for me, Tobias?"

He lowered his head. He sat completely still and stared at his knees.

She thought she might be getting somewhere. "Why not?" she asked.

He swallowed. "Aw, man," he said, shaking his head. "Can't believe you're still mad about stuff that happened thirty-some years ago."

Her eyes were moist. "Do I look angry?"

"Well, it sounds like it. Y'know that's nuts, right?"

"Is it? I remember *everything*. Every mean thing you said. I don't claim to be the picture of mental health, but I don't have dementia either."

His eye twitched. "Wow. Didn't know we had such a complicated relationship." He smirked.

"Being condescending is how you want to deal with this? Really?"

"I'm not, Maddie. Seriously, I have nuthin' but nice memories. Some people focus on the bad stuff and some hang onto the good. I'm in the good stuff camp. Man. Does Lisa know you got all this baggage? 'Cause when I've asked about you she never said anything."

"Lisa never told me you asked about me."

"Of course I did. Over the years. I know you sing. You toured with some big act. Whitney Houston, I think, right? Still married?"

Maddie ran her right hand over the fingers on her left. She shook her head.

"Oh. Me neither. Y'ever ask her about *me*?"

She shrugged.

"Oh yeah?" He grinned with his cheeks puffed up like

he used to when he was a kid. "Well, Maddie, wish I had time to rethink my childhood and recall all the stuff you do. Maybe someday. For now, I got a full time job, middle-age back pain, a dying dad, bitter ex-wife, and a depressed teenager. My sister's dodging bullets and bombs in Iraq. Mom's gone AWOL with some guy whose name I don't even know. Got enough to keep me cryin', so I try not to think about sad stuff I don't need to be thinking about. I'd like to buy you a beer down at Fisherman's Feast and look across the table at your frozen-in-time face. But please don't expect me to remember something I said or didn't say when I was six, or twelve, or even twenty-five. I don't remember what the hell I said last week. Last night."

"Fisherman's Feast?" she said. "I wouldn't go there."

"You kiddin'? That's the *spot*. Been around since before we were born."

"Isn't it a redneck bar?"

"Redneck? Uh, y'know that word's not okay, right? I've done sensitivity training, believe it or not. Redneck is a slur."

"Oh. Really? I always thought people were proud to be rednecks."

"Not everyone."

"Sorry. I don't drink beer. Only red wine."

"Ah. Fancy."

"It has resveratrol. It's anti-aging."

"So, you'll join me if they have red wine?"

She lifted her shoulders and dropped them. "You sure they allow Black people in there?"

He smiled.

"Well do they?" she asked.

He laughed.

The sunset streaked the clouds pink-gold and orange as the bus moved past the waterfall, around the pond, and then under the Christmas garland hanging above the center of town. Old snow clung in patches along the water banks on either side of Lake Street. They turned and stopped at the storefront depot on Millpond Parkway.

The Kangol guy got off ahead of Tobias and Maddie. Through the window, she saw her mother in her silver Mercedes station wagon parked alongside the pond across the street. Velma looked through her back window and waved at Kangol cap. He waved back. Interesting, Maddie thought. She used to know *all* the Black people in Monroe. All five of them. Including her.

"Think your mom would give me a ride?" Tobias asked as they stepped off the bus.

"Depends what kind of mood she's in."

He pulled her over-packed luggage from under the bus, while her mother popped the lock. Maddie opened the rear hatch. Velma turned toward her from behind the wheel as Bertold growled from the back seat. Tobias made an *oof* sound as he lifted her suitcase into the station wagon. Maddie set her backpack beside it.

"Jesus, Maddie. You moving back home?" her mother said, laughing.

"Thanks for coming to get me. Could we give Tobias a ride to his dad's?"

Velma's smile vanished. She hadn't noticed who was helping her with the bag until then. "I guess," she said.

"Thank you." Maddie turned to Tobias. "Don't touch the dog. He's mean."

She got in the front next to her mother and he climbed into the back with Bertold, who stunk up the whole car with a funk that reminded Maddie of toe jam.

"Thanks, Mrs. Arrington. How you been?"

"Well, gettin' old's not the greatest and my cholesterol's 290, but I'm still here. How's your father?"

"Still here, too, last time I checked," he said. "He's on his way out, though."

"Aren't we all?" Velma said.

Maddie winced and looked back at Tobias. Bertold climbed into his lap.

"No, no. Don't let him sit on you. Mom, tell the dog to get down."

"He's fine," Velma said.

Tobias screwed up his face the way one does when something stinks so bad you want to retch. He patted the dog's head gingerly with two fingers as if he worried he might catch something.

Velma drove along the length of the pond toward Tobias's dad's house. A few Mallards swam in the center.

"When we were kids," Maddie said, "the pond used to be frozen solid this time of year. We skated on it. Remember?"

"Yeah," Velma said. "And ducks used to fly south. The weather's topsy-turvy. It's crazy."

"You all don't believe in that global warming crap," Tobias said. "Do you?"

Maddie heard Bertold growl.

Then Tobias shrieked, "OOW!"

"What happened?" Velma said.

"Little bastard bit me!" The dog jumped to the floor and cowered behind Maddie's seat.

"What'd you do to him?" Velma yelled. The tires screeched as she pulled over just before they got to the waterfall.

"Nothing. He fuckin' bit me in the face for no reason." Tobias leaned forward to look at his cheek in the rearview mirror. "Does he have all his shots?"

"Should we go to the hospital?" Maddie asked.

"Of course he has all his shots," Velma snapped. "Why wouldn't he?" She turned the ceiling light on and examined Tobias's face. "You'll be fine. Just put some peroxide on it. BERTOLD. GET UP HERE, YOU BAD DOG." She reached back, snatched him up by his harness, and plopped him into Maddie's lap.

"I don't want him!" She covered her face with her forearms.

Velma lifted him off Maddie's lap. "Well then get in

the back."

She climbed out, and then into the back seat beside Tobias. He sat there with his hand on his face, too angry to look at her. No one spoke.

The graveled driveway of Tobias and Maddie's childhood was now a smooth blacktop. They pulled in front of the green house with white trim. Tobias jumped out and slung his backpack over his shoulder.

"See you at the funeral?" Maddie asked.

"I'm reporting the dog." He slammed the door and walked away.

Maddie got out and opened the front passenger door. "Can you put your monster in the back again, please?"

Velma huffed, but she did pick Bertold up and set him down behind the front seat. When Maddie sank down and closed the door, her mother backed out of the driveway and peeled off. "Screw him," she said. "I'm glad Bertold bit him."

"You really are insane. You know that?"

"Can't stand that kid," Velma said.

Maddie's eyebrows inched up. Had her mother held a grudge, too? "Because of what happened almost forty years ago?"

"What, Maddie? What is it you think happened?"

Velma was driving really fast and to Maddie, she seemed angrier than she needed to be.

"He called me the N-word," she said.

"Oh, who gives a sugar shake about that? You

remember why his parents split up?"

"No. I never knew why. And I don't care. It's none of my business."

"His mother moved away shortly after your father went off with that bow-wow who used to be his patient. That was one scandal. Okay. The other was the rumor that Tobias might not be Dan's son. You getting the picture now?"

"No."

Velma exhaled. "Madeline, your father couldn't keep himself off any slut in this town who'd stand still for two minutes. He's so stupid he'd step over fillet mignon to pick up a Big Mac."

"Wait. Are you saying—"

"Yes."

Maddie gave Velma the look Velma had given her all her life when something sounded like some bullshit. Eyes that're so onto your nonsense they don't even have to roll. Lips set into the opposite of a smile. "That's preposterous," she said. "You didn't even move to this neighborhood until you were pregnant with me and Tobias and I are the same age."

"Your father was working up here already. They could've met."

"You'd pull anything out of your ass to disparage my father. You once told me he was gay."

"You don't know that he isn't."

"So he's a *gay* womanizer?"

"There *was* a man I think he slept with."

"Oh, Mom, just be quiet."

"He disparaged himself when he disrespected his wife to chase after these bitches up here. This is a small town, Maddie. People know all your business."

"On my twenty-fourth birthday you told me he didn't want to have me."

"Well, he didn't. Your father had your half sister. He didn't want any more kids."

"And you *had* to tell me that? On my birthday?"

Velma stared at the road.

"While it wouldn't surprise me if Dad had a kid I didn't know about, I'm pretty positive he didn't sire Tobias."

"You don't know."

"First of all, we couldn't be related to anyone who doesn't believe in climate change. And as much as he's complained about being 'daughtered out'? He'd claim a son if he had one."

Velma looked at her. "I was pregnant once after you, y'know? Would've been a boy. He didn't want it."

"Mom, shut up."

"Your father's an asshole."

"Watch the road."

The Presbyterian Church stood boldly in the center of town. It was a white wooden structure with four proud columns in the front and a tall steeple housing a bell that sounded like joy when it rang. It had been there since the mid-nineteenth century. Iris's family, before she married, had worshipped there for generations. As a kid, Maddie played at the waterfall just up the street. The whoosh of the water mixed with the ringing bell was a sonic delight and helped her imagine magical places she would one day go.

Lisa married here twenty years earlier. The bell sang its happy song as they showered her and her groom with white rose petals. Maddie was a bridesmaid and the Arringtons were the only Black family there. That morning while Velma flat-ironed her hair in the bathroom, Maddie asked her, "Do you think the Megnas could be passing?"

Their eyes met in the mirror. "Why would you ask that?" Velma said.

"Well, they treat us like family. Just wondering."

Her mother's eyes rolled heavenward and she blew air through her lips, making them vibrate. "No, Maddie. They're not passing. They were good neighbors when we lived next door and so were we, and that's why we're still friends. You don't think white people can be nice? What's wrong with you?"

Today the bells were silent as they climbed the concrete steps, past the green shrubs with chunks of snow laid on them like thin bricks. They entered through the tall double doors. Velma wore a dark gray skirt suit under her mink, and Maddie was in a black wool dress and a velvet coat that Velma had warned her wasn't going to be warm enough. She was right. Maddie's teeth chattered as Bobby Ferrell greeted them with programs in hand. He was tall, fit, with a thick head of silver, and his suit was well made. It looked like life had been good to him. This prompted a string of obscenities to glide through Maddie's mind like a song.

"I'm still so sad about your father, dear," Velma told Bobby. "I'll miss him."

"Thank you, Velma." He kissed her cheek.

"Close your mouth, Maddie," her mother said. "Bobby's my customer. He used to come down to the shop with his dad."

He smiled at Maddie as he walked the two of them down the aisle between the pews. "How are you, Maddie?"

She didn't answer. She pictured him as he'd been locked in her memory, sneering, threatening, hurling slurs.

"Bobby's the town historian now," Velma said.

"Bobby threw rocks at me and called me a ni—."

"—Ooh, good God!" Velma groaned. "Would you let it go?"

Bobby stopped at a pew and extended a hand, gesturing for them to sit. He eased out a breath. "She's right," he said. He averted his eyes for a moment before looking Maddie straight in the face. "I have a nine-year-old and I'd be ashamed if he behaved the way I did. He wouldn't. He's been raised to respect everyone. Things were different back then, Maddie. We didn't know better." He reached out and touched her shoulder.

Maddie jerked away and turned toward the pew.

Her mother moved in front of her and slid in beside a plump old woman whose thighs easily took up two seats. She wore a long, frosted blond wig that was too youthful for her double-chinned face etched with trenches around the eyes and mouth. Maddie slid down next to her mother.

"Hi Velma," the wrinkled woman said with a smoker's husky voice.

"How are you, Sally? Your husband doing okay, dear?"

In that moment, Maddie's world flipped on its head.

Velma Arrington was being friendly with the raving racist *Sally Gore*? The woman once slammed the door in Maddie's face when she was selling Girl Scout cookies. "Get away from here and don't you come back," she had said. "I wouldn't buy a water hose from you people if my house was on fire."

"Velma, I'm ready to kill myself," Sally croaked. "Pete sleeps all day, then at night he prowls the house and eats every damn thing in the kitchen. I hadda chain lock the refrigerator. And the pantry too. Middle of the night last week he drove down to Fisherman's Feast in his pajamas, no shoes on, in the freezing cold and the idiot bartender let him run up a tab before they called me. Now I gotta hide the friggin' car keys, too!"

Velma made a sympathetic face and patted Sally in a consoling way on her large thigh.

The organ began a melancholy whine. Maddie opened the program, and saw a picture of herself and Lisa. They were seven, in Halloween bunny costumes. Mrs. Megna, blond and gorgeous like a supermodel, knelt between them, with her arms around their shoulders. She flipped the page and noticed the name "Madeline Arrington" in a flowery font. According to the program, she was singing "Amazing Grace."

Stunned, she pointed at it, to show her mother.

"Oh yeah. I forgot to tell you," Velma said.

"WHAT?"

"I figured you'd want to sing."

"You crazy old lady," Maddie hissed, "What the fuck is wrong with you?"

Velma gritted her teeth and narrowed her eyes. "Don't call me that. And watch your mouth, we're in a church."

"I don't remember the goddamn words to Amazing Grace," Maddie whisper-shrieked. "And I don't know what key I sing it in!"

"SShhh," Velma hissed. "The words are right in the program. What're you, blind?"

Sally Gore glowered at Maddie. Maddie wanted to punch them both.

After the pastor gave the opening prayer, it was her cue. As Maddie approached the lectern, she gazed out at the sea of faces. There was Lisa, red haired and quietly beautiful, and her older brothers, raven haired like their dad had been. They sat in the front with their spouses, their kids in the row behind. Her eyes sailed across the crowd of at least a hundred people; large, considering it was New Year's Eve. She couldn't spot Tobias. She hoped his face was okay. And then she sang:

"Amazing grace, how sweet the sound
That saved a wretch like me."

Though Maddie loved how the song rolled off the vocal cords, never would she sing it of her own volition. Its composer was a slave trader who wrote it after decades of making money by abusing Africans—selling them, and treating them as subhuman.

"I once was lost, but now am found,
Was blind, but now I see."

The acoustics danced with her voice, swirling and thrumming it in concentric circles that billowed out and filled the sanctuary. Stellar. Still, she asked herself, *what am I doing standing in this white church in this white town that crushed my spirit, singing the words of a white supremacist who wrote it for his own forgiveness? Why should I forgive?*

"'Twas grace that taught my heart to fear ..."

She saw that her mother's wasn't the only face of color in the crowd. There were others, not a lot, maybe eight.

Some Latinos and Asians, too. If the complexion of the town was changing, were attitudes changing as well, like Bobby suggested? Was she the only one weighed down by the past like the low end of a seesaw? Why *can't* I let it go? She wondered.

"And grace my fears relieved."

Singing magnified every feeling. Resentment for this place had worked its way into the deepest pockets of her soul. Yet there was love stuffed down there, too, for old friends, some of them sitting right in front of her. The Megnas' loss bled into her own and the combined grief swelled and ached in Maddie's chest. It began to seep into her voice. *Relax, breathe. Think of something else.* The emotion kept rising. She couldn't quell it.

"How precious did that grace appear,<br>
The hour I first believed."

Finally, a dam broke inside her, and a river of unresolved anguish gushed out. Maddie tried to relax her throat. It didn't work. She couldn't think ahead or form words or hit notes. Crying may have been apropos; it was a funeral. But the sobbing while singing made the moment about her, which was not cool. Through the blur of tears she saw wide eyes, and gaping mouths on a number of faces, some red and contorted with sobs of their own. Her mother rested her face in her hands.

Lisa stood. "It's okay," she said. She began to sing the next verse.

"Through many dangers, toils and snares,"

Her brothers Matthew and Anthony joined her.

"We have already come;"

Their spouses and their kids chimed in, as well. Soon almost everyone in the church was singing, including Sally Gore, and Bobby, and one of his brothers.

"'Tis grace has brought me safe thus far,
And grace will lead me home."

They were doing this for Iris, of course. But standing there before the townies singing right at her, their voices a whirl of divine acoustics, it felt like being hugged by a hundred souls.

Walking to the car after the service, Velma said, "Jesus, I really should've told you. That was awful, oh my God." Her hands clapped onto her cheeks.

Maddie wasn't sure if the temperature had risen or if her body heat had. Her neck was hot and her feet were tired. "Where's the repast?" she asked.

Velma popped the locks on her station wagon. "They don't call it that here. Where d'you think you are, Harlem?"

Maddie hissed out a breath as she opened the

passenger door. "Whatever the hell they call it. Just tell me where we're going!"

"Stop yelling at me. The *reception* is at Liser's."

Velma drove past the waterfall and up the hill. Maddie looked out the window at the old neighborhood. Holiday lights on the houses sparkled and shined. Velma went beyond the golf course and looped around to give the Megnas time to get home.

The three-story white house was next door to the one Maddie's parents sold when she was fourteen. Lisa's husband had moved in after they married two decades earlier. They never left.

Maddie hugged Lisa at the door. Her friend's body was a warm cushion. The few extra pounds she'd put on over the years looked pretty on her and she smelled sweet, like Marzipan.

"So sorry about the song."

Lisa squeezed her tighter. "No, it was good. We needed you to get the crying going." She sniffled. "Means a lot that you're here, Mad. Thanks for coming."

"I loved your mom. Love you too, Patty-Lisa."

While Velma greeted Lisa next, Maddie hugged her kids and met the nieces and nephews. One of the boys, a short ten-year-old with shaggy, strawberry blond hair and cheeks like juicy peaches said, "No offense, but I don't think you should sing at any more funerals."

Maddie smiled briefly and then bellowed, "Thanks for the advice." She glared at Velma, who looked over.

"Yeah, yeah. Blame her mother," Velma told the kid. "Blame me for *everything*, like she does."

Maddie's heels tapped across the oak floor as she walked away. Her eyes swept around the living room and the dining room as guests continued to arrive. No Tobias. Through the front window, his father's house twinkled across the street, draped in yellow lights. She pulled her Palm Treo from her purse to call him and then realized his number wasn't in it. She saw that Sam had texted: *Missing your delicious red velvet voice. Hurry back.*

There was a flutter.

Lisa's house didn't have a front driveway; it was in the back. Tobias's house was down the hill in the front, which meant Maddie had to sidestep, carefully, to descend her former double-diamond-ski-slope-steep driveway in her heels.

An evergreen wreath circled the brass knocker on the front door. Tobias was smiling when he opened it. He had on a well-worn blue sweatshirt and his cheek bore four tiny holes surrounded by red, inflamed skin. Maddie heard his father's laughter coming from the living room.

"Hi. Came to see if you wanted to join us at Lisa's."

"In a bit. Come in for a minute."

Tomato sauce with basil filled the air when she stepped inside. She smelled pine, too. Their tree, at the other end of the room, near the hallway, was tiny, but its fragrance was real. Maddie waved at Tobias's dad in the recliner. He was watching *The 40-Year-Old Virgin* on a large woodgrain TV.

"Hello, Mr. Milton."

He waved back without taking his eyes off the movie. Completely bald, he wore big, black-framed eyeglasses, and he was covered up to his neck with a brown and white crocheted afghan. Mr. Milton laughed and laughed.

"He's in good spirits for a dying person," she whispered to Tobias.

He sat on the brown corduroy sofa, looked at her, and then patted the cushion beside him. She sat far enough to be unable to touch him with her thigh, but close enough that she could have reached him with her hand.

"He doesn't want any stress around him," Tobias explained. "He just wants to watch funny stuff, which is good for me, 'cause I can't be pissed off when I'm here. He won't stand for it. Right, Pop?" Tobias turned to her. "I was screaming at my son on the phone one night and he told me to stop it or leave. I didn't stop fast enough and he went and called the cops on me. Can you believe that? He told 'em to escort me out."

"Good. Does that mean you can't be mad about that?" She pointed at his swollen cheek.

His smile deadpanned. He was mad.

"So sorry. How's it feeling?" she asked.

"I guess I'll live."

"Did you put some antibacterial ointment on it?"

"Maddie, how 'bout, I let this go, and you let your stuff go?"

She glanced up at the popcorn ceiling, before her eyes landed on the movie. It was the scene where Catherine Keener's character is on her way to Andy's apartment and Seth Rogan explains why that's terrible, because his place is filled with a billion toys. He needs to grow up.

"Well?" Tobias said.

"Let it go where? Where do I send it?"

"Just don't, y'know, hold it against me."

"I told you I'm not angry."

He squinted at her, doubtful. His dad laughed at the TV.

"Do you remember magic kisses?" she asked.

He closed his eyes for a moment. When he opened them they brightened. "For boo-boos? Yeah. *Magic kisses, your hurt has disappeared.*"

"Yes. You were a sweet little boy. My Tobias."

His dark eyes rested on hers. They glistened. His cheeks flushed.

Outside, someone yelled, "Pete! You better get back in the house! Come here."

"Pete Gore's loose again, sounds like," Mr. Milton mumbled.

"Uh, jeeze," Tobias said. He stood up and peered out the front window. Then he opened the door.

A thin, elderly Mr. Gore, frail, with patchy gray hair, scampered in, barefoot, wearing dark blue pajamas. "Help me," he squealed, ducking behind Mr. Milton's chair. "That old hag is trying to catch me!"

Tobias smiled. "Mr. Gore, don't talk that way about your wife."

Sally Gore barreled into the doorway, breathing heavily. Her blonde wig was gone. Wispy white hair hung down to her saggy chin. She wore a gray wool coat, gray sweatpants with cinched elastic at the ankles, and purple moccasins with no socks.

Mr. Gore recoiled. "My wife? That's not my *wife*. I don't even know that ugly witch."

Tobias's face twisted into a Picasso. His lips pursed and stretched to the side. One black piano key brow sprang up toward his hairline, the other smashed against the bridge of his nose. An eye bulged like a giggle was trying to shove it out of the way.

"Pete, get over here now!" Sally yelled as she stomped toward him. Her bare ankles were thick and purplish and bumpy with veins.

"Stay away from me, woman. I'm trying to get to work!"

"You don't friggin' work anymore. You're retired."

Mr. Milton paused the movie with his remote. He adjusted his glasses, crossed his arms and watched the Gores with amusement. Tobias turned his reddened face to the wall.

Maddie was entertained, too, though only briefly. She looked at Mr. Gore and he looked at her.

He gasped. "Did she break in?" His head swung toward Mr. Milton. "She shouldn't be here." He pointed at her. "She's a nigger."

"Ah-ah. Nope, no," Mr. Milton scolded. "I don't like that kind of talk, Pete."

Sally clapped both hands over her mouth as her husband bent at the waist and charged at Maddie like a bull.

Maddie leapt off the couch, out of his path. Her heartbeat drummed in her throat.

Tobias dove after Mr. Gore, grabbed him from behind and brought his skinny body to the beige carpeted floor.

"Oh-oh," Sally shouted. "Please be careful. His bones are brittle."

"Get off me," the old man yelled. "You can't let 'em in your house."

"Sorry," Sally said to Maddie. "He's got Alzheimer's. Don't listen to him. He doesn't know what he's talking about."

Maddie humphed to herself. *Sure he doesn't.*

Tobias helped Mr. Gore up onto the couch. "You all right, sir?"

"No, you cocksucker. That hurt!"

"I didn't mean to. But I couldn't let you assault my friend." He held him by the arm.

"That's your *friend*?" Mr. Gore grimaced at Maddie as if she were a stinking puddle of puke.

"Yeah. And you leave her alone, you hear? Or it'll hurt more the next time." Tobias's eyes found Maddie's.

The warm look that passed between them was quick

and quiet and anyone watching might have missed it. But it meant something to Maddie that Tobias had her back.

Mr. Gore hung his head and shook it. A patch of silver-gray strands fell forward onto his lined forehead. "Nobody's worried about niggers no more."

Maddie almost laughed.

*This* was where she was from.

The voice of this place had been loud and she'd carried it with her all her life. Now she saw that the voice was nothing but a beat-down, demented, old fossil clinging to the need to be better, because its own image was so fragile.

Tobias turned to Sally. "You can open the closet and grab him a coat. The sneakers from last time are in that basket at the bottom."

"I'll help you," Maddie said. She followed Sally, who lumbered toward the closet door on her thick legs. When she opened it, Maddie reached down and picked up a pair of worn out white tennis shoes. "These?"

"Thank you." Sally spoke softly and didn't look at her.

Maddie thought she seemed chastened. She brought the old shoes to Tobias and watched as he scooted down and put them on Mr. Gore's bare feet. The skin was so thin and white it looked translucent. She watched Tobias and Sally help the old man up. They gently guided his arms into the coat.

Mr. Milton pointed the DVD remote at the TV and resumed his movie.

"Be back soon, Pop," Tobias chimed.

His dad grunted.

Maddie said goodbye and he didn't respond. He was smiling at the TV, fully enjoying the last drops of his life. Maybe it was just that simple, she thought. Stop resisting, and find ways to be happy. She followed the trio outside.

Tobias and Sally flanked Mr. Gore, each clenching one of his upper arms. A motion detector light blinked on and bathed the driveway in a glow. Maddie's heels clicked a few paces behind them as they headed toward the street. Her teeth chattered from the cold. "Hey, Mrs. Gore," she said.

"What?" Sally didn't look back.

"I appreciate you saying you're sorry."

The old lady's purple moccasins kept scuffing along the blacktop. She didn't turn around. Mr. Gore did. He peeked over his shoulder at Maddie and stuck out his tongue. Then he sang, "NiggAR!" He actually *sang* it. On "G."

"Shut up, Pete." Sally shook his arm.

"*You* shut up. You big-old hag," Mr. Gore said.

Tobias turned and made cross-eyes at Maddie before facing foward again.

"I'm surprised, though," Maddie said, speaking to Sally. "Because you called me the same thing when I was a kid. You hated 'us people'." She was still behind the three of them as they reached the edge of the driveway. "Now you're friendly with my mother? What changed?"

Sally Gore stopped moving, forcing Tobias and Mr. Gore to stop as well. She kept her grip on her husband's arm as she turned toward Maddie. Her thin lips were a crescent moon tipped over. "Been a *long* time since you were a kid. You're old, and I got less life ahead of me than I got behind. I didn't know anyone who wasn't white, growing up. No one."

"NiggAAAR!" Mr. Gore sang.

Maddie bit back the urge to sing, *crackAAR*!

Sally exhaled. "Neither did he." She closed the top button on her coat. "And what'd'you think I heard about anybody who wasn't like us?" She raised her brows above weary eyes and then she shrugged. "We believed it. What else did we know?"

"NiggAR!"

"Oh, Pete, please," Sally groaned.

"His voice is delightful," Maddie said, though it wasn't.

Sally nodded. "He was a tenor in the church choir."

"Great."

"I gotta get him home. G'night, Maddie," she said, turning to leave. "You take good care. Happy New Year."

"Yeah. Same to you. Out with the old."

"See you at Lisa's," Tobias yelled over his shoulder.

Maddie watched them head down the street and fade into the dark like dissipating ghosts.

Her feet were freezing, sore too, in those heels. They carried her in the opposite direction. Despite the pain, instead of heading back up the hill to Lisa's house, she walked down to the waterfall.

When she got there, she touched the metal railing along the sidewalk that kept pedestrians and cars from plunging into the stream several yards below. She leaned into the metal and listened to the thrum of tumbling water, the rush of the torrent. Sounded like the energy of life itself, thundering on, unstoppable. It goes so fast, she thought. But it had also run long enough for her to see that no matter what she did, whether she succeeded or failed, whether she got it, or she didn't, life continued. It was perpetually in motion. And things did change.

Her Treo rang.

"Hi, Mom."

"Maddie! Where the hell are you? Been looking all over for you. Did you leave? You won't believe what I just heard. Remember that teacher who called you a liar when you told him we'd been to Japan? Well, he *died*."

"Be there in a minute, Mom."

"Last month. Don't know how I missed it. Didn't see it in the paper."

"Mom."

"So, you can let *that* grudge go, 'cause he's—"

Maddie tapped the button with her cold fingers to turn down the volume. And as she did, the phone slipped from her grasp. She watched it plummet into the stream.

Out with the old.

She stared at the water rushing by beneath her,

listening to it fall and flow. She listened to the passing cars, moving like a current toward the end of the year and into the beginning of a new one.

In the next phase, maybe she'd enjoy the good more. Maybe she'd get better at letting things go, and at riding out the bad.

She would try again.

Her feet still hurt. One step in front of the other, she walked up the hill anyway, because this was her life, the journey continued, and she wanted to see where it would take her.

## *ACKNOWLEDGMENTS*

Working with Accents Publishing has been a dream! Thank you, Katerina Stoykova, for creating the novella contest, and for choosing *Homegoing* as the winner. It's been a pleasure to move through this process with you. I'm so fortunate to have received your encouragement, guidance, and enthusiasm. You're a generous editor and publisher. I've enjoyed getting to know your work as writer and as an actress as well. You are endlessly inspiring!

Thanks also to my awesome agent, Dara Hyde. *Homegoing* exists because of your interest in the many stories you've encouraged me to keep working over the past several years.

My writing community could not be more wonderful. The kindness and support I receive from so many writer friends and colleagues amazes me. You've been there through ups and downs, and I appreciate each of you immensely. A few people offered specific help and support for *Homegoing*.

Devin Galaudet—thank you for inviting me to read during the launch of your fabulous memoir, *10,000 Miles with my Dead Father's Ashes*. It was the first time I read publicly from this book and that experience was invaluable. Tisha Marie Reichle-Aguilera, thank you so much for your continual support for this manuscript, and for telling me about the Faulkner Society contest. Placing as a semi-finalist was a boost that inspired me to keep working. Kate Maruyama, I *so* depend on your super smart notes. They never fail to leave me eager to approach the next draft. You're the greatest!

I'm also grateful for the support of: Nana-Ama Danquah, Nicole Sconiers, David Rocklin, Jeff Stetson, Ann Marsh, Debralyn Press, Stuart Dybek, Nina Lorenz Collins, Aya de Leon, Colette Sartor, Pamela Mshana, Nathan Gonzalez, Jacinda Townsend, and Alma Luz Villanueva.

And thanks to Leonard Chang for everything.

## *ABOUT THE AUTHOR*

Toni Ann Johnson's novel *Remedy For a Broken Angel* was nominated for a 2015 NAACP Image Award for Outstanding Literary Work by a Debut Author. She won the 2015 International Latino Book Award for Most Inspirational Fiction. Her stage plays have been produced by The Negro Ensemble Company (co-author "Here in My Father's House"), The New York Stage and Film Company ("Gramercy Park is Closed to the Public"), and in Los Angeles by The Fountainhead Theatre Company.

Johnson is the recipient of two Humanitas Prizes and a Christopher Award for her screenplays *Ruby Bridges*, for Disney / ABC and *Crown Heights*, for Showtime Television. She wrote the Fox Television pilot *Save The Last Dance* and she co-wrote the feature film *Step Up 2: The Streets*. Johnson's essays and short fiction have appeared in *The Los Angeles Times*, *The Emerson Review*, *Hunger Mountain*, *Xavier Review*, *Callaloo Journal*, and elsewhere. She's been a Sundance Screenwriter's Lab Fellow, as well as a Callaloo Fellow in fiction at Brown University. Johnson has received additional support for her writing from The Prague Summer Program for Writers and the One-Story Summer Conference in Brooklyn. She teaches screenwriting at The University of Southern California.

CPSIA information can be obtained
at www.ICGtesting.com
Printed in the USA
BVHW071044010621
608543BV00002B/356